Daddy's Naughty Baby

An ABDL age play romantic love story about a naughty baby girl who learned that her Daddy Dom could surprise her in more kinky DDLG ways than one

By Tina Moore

Table of Contents

Chapter 1

Lola got dressed in the short pink dress that had taken 26 shifts at the hardware store to afford. She zipped up the back, carefully pulled on her black heels, doing the buckle up at the ankle. Taking one final look in the mirror, she smirked.

"Tonight is going to be amazing," she said out loud as she ran her fingers through her straight blonde hair. Grabbing her clutch on the way out of the house, she double checked to make sure she had the invitation, her strawberry chapstick and the clip Jake had bought her for her hair. He had told her he wanted to put it in her hair and to wait for him by the door of their high school building.

"I am pleased to present the Homecoming King and Queen of 2009, Jake Hudson and Lola

Price," the school Principle of Fever Tree High said down the microphone. The student body cheered, Jake took Lola's hand, and they danced as though everything in their world's finally made sense.

That night was over ten years ago, and nothing more than a distant memory as Lola packed up her truck, securing the ropes over her cupboard which was laying in the tray.

"This'll be the last load; after this, let's get a drink!" She called from the tray. Lola had cut the ties of her small town country roots and bolted like an untrained Brumby out of her home town the minute she had turned 21. She only had one direction on her mind, Hollywood. It had been harder for her to break into the scene than she had first thought, and with nothing more than a changed dream and a plan to make it work, she was coming home.

"Good. I still can't believe you want to go home. It's not like you haven't made a name for yourself. Sure you aren't some big movie star, but you've had constant, well-paying work for years now. That's more than most of us can say," her friend Kate said, wiping the sweat from her brow.

"Yeah, I know, but it's time. Living here has been fun, but I want something - I can't believe I'm about to say this - a little more homegrown," Lola replied, climbing into the drivers' seat.

"Ready?" Kate asked, sensing Lola's hesitation. Lola just looked straight ahead and smiled as she looked down the road.

"Ready," she said as she pulled out and began her final trip home.

"Hey man, what's up?" Jake said, shaking hands with the owner of the home he was building. Jake had gone into the construction business, making his way up the ranks from apprentice to project manager. As an established businessman with a strong portfolio of success, he had branched out on his own and started his company three years ago. With his country morals and cowboy manner, it had not been surprising to the town that his company was one of the best performers. He had successfully redesigned the city, modernizing it yet holding onto its heritage foundation, taking it from a drive-by location to a luxury country hot stop, creating a steady flow of tourism.

"Can't complain, won't change anything," the homeowner replied, making Jake laugh.

"Hey, have you heard Lola is coming back home?" The man said, causing Jake to lift his eyebrow in surprise.

"That's not a name I've heard for a while," Jake replied, making the man laugh and slap his back.

"Heard you two used to drive by the river," the man said signing the papers Jake had brought for him.

"Something like that," Jake muttered, remembering how he had held Lola through the night on more than one occasion.

"Well, she's hauled up at her Daddy's. Heard her Mama talking about it downtown. Might be worth passing by, Lord knows you could use a woman. You still talk to Marg Wilson's girl, Tammy?" The man asked, but Jake hardly heard a word as he remembered Lola's sweet green eyes looking up at him like he could save the world.

"What? Argh, no. Thanks for this. I've got to go," Jake said, rolling up the plans and the signed paperwork before shaking the man's hand again and turning swiftly.

"Yeah, you go get her," the man yelled, laughing as Jake climbed into his truck.

Jake drove through tree-lined streets, acknowledging the locals he passed with a casual flick of his hand or tilt of his head. He wasn't sure what he was going to say to Lola; all Jake knew was that he needed to see her. And see her he did! Jumping down from her done-up black truck with the extra wide rims, Jake saw her tanned legs complemented by brown and turquoise cowgirl boots that kicked the dust up when she landed two feet first.

"Damn," Jake muttered his breath, placing both hands in his pockets and leaning forward slightly in his seat as he exhaled. He had parked his truck across the street from Lola's Father's house and watched as her slender arms flexed when she lifted a box that was too heavy for her. Opening the door of his truck, Jake jumped down and crossed the road, the look in his eyes burning with lust.

"Howdy, can I give you ladies a hand?" Jake said, tipping his hat and slowly lifting his head to look Lola in the eye.

"Depends, where do you think we'd want you?" Lola smartly said back, causing Jake to smile involuntarily.

"How about here," Jake said, reaching under Lola's hands and taking the box from her and walking it inside. Lola eyed him, not surprised that he was still in town. When she had left for the city, she had waited for him by the welcoming sigh on the border of their town for three hours before deciding that he wasn't coming. She had turned on the ignition of her old beat up station-wagon and never looked back. That was until today. Today she was looking at a ghost who had undoubtedly become even more handsome than she remembered him being.

"How are you?" Lola said as Jake walked back out to her truck. He had tried to refrain from looking at her face until now; now, he had no choice. Her long waves of blonde hair, and lips that looked like they had a secret that they just needed to tell made him wonder why he had let her go.

"Yeah good. You?" Jake said, his hazel eyes sparkling the way Lola remembered they did.

"You want to get out of here?" Lola asked, taking Jake's hand in hers as though no time had passed between them. As though Jake hadn't broken her heart, and as though Jake's heart still didn't belong to her.

"Yeah, I know a place," Jake said, as Lola's friend, Kate walked back inside seeing the almost intoxicating chemistry between the two.

"Same old Jake," Lola said, seeing that he had taken her to their old spot by the river. Jake just turned the truck off and sat in the driver's seat, feeling more out of control than he had in ten years. Lola looked at him before turning to look out over the river. The day had been sunny, not a cloud in the sky, and the water was glistening with the sun's reflection.

"Remember this," Lola asked softly, for the first time showing him the side of her he had loved too much.

"I remember everything, baby," Jake said as a tear rolled down his cheek.

"I'm sorry I wasn't there for you when you needed me the most," Jake said, wiping the tear away and turning to face Lola. The plan had been to leave together, to start a new life after Lola's sister had died in a freak car crash four days before Lola's 19th birthday. Jake remembered how she had run to his house in the middle of the night and banged on the front door, so loudly the neighbors had called the cops.

"It doesn't matter. I got over it, even found someone new," Lola said, remembering how she had cried in his arms, wrapped in her favorite pink fluffy blankie as her heart broke into pieces that would never heal.

"Someone new?" Jake asked, looking for a wedding ring on her finger. Lola just laughed.

"It's not that far yet, and I don't think it will ever be," she replied, taking Jake's hand in hers and holding it to her heart.

"Not everyone can be my Daddy," Lola said, her wicked grin spreading across her face and eyes catching the first rays of moonlight.

"No?" Jake teased.

"No, Daddy," Lola whispered in Jake's ear, leaning over and pressing her breasts against his arm making him smirk.

"You were always such a playfully little thing, Lola," he said, cupping her chin in his hand and looking into her eyes, watching her as she nodded her head slowly. Leaning forward, Jake pressed his lips to hers, sighing in relief for the first time in years as he tasted her strawberry chapstick once again.

"Daddy," Lola whispered against his lips, causing Jake to open his eyes and see her smiling.

"I've missed you, baby girl," Jake said, leaning back and stroking the side of her face.

"I can see that," Lola giggled, looking at how hard Jake was, his cock pushing firmly against his jeans. Placing her hand on his belt buckle, Lola pulled on it teasingly.

"Let Daddy help you, baby girl," Jake said, unbuckling his belt and unzipping his pants. Lola watched as his cock sprung from his jeans, pulsating with anticipation.

"Do you still like it like this, Daddy?" Lola said, teasing him by slowly licking up his hard shaft. Jake gently grabbed the back of her head and positioned her mouth over the tip and slowly slid into her mouth.

"Yeah, baby girl, time to be a good girl for me," Jake said, in a hoarse voice as he felt her throat open for him. Lola tried to reach for him, but Jake took her arms and pinned them behind her back as he thrust into her mouth, making her head bouncing up and down on his rod.

"You're going to swallow all of Daddy, do you understand, little one?" Jake said as he felt his cock exploded with cum into Lola's mouth. Lola just nodded her head as she was restrained and face fucked, dripping cum from her lips and onto Jake's lap. He didn't care, he hadn't had her for years, and as she gagged on his hard cock, Jake knew he had to have more of her.

"Come here," Jake said, suddenly pulling Lola off him and reaching up her skirt and into her panties.

"Such a smooth little girl, do you want Daddy to play in here little one?" Jake said, pushing a finger into Lola's mouth and making her suck it before gently parting her pussy lips and sliding his wet finger up and down her warm, soft pussy.

"Yes, Daddy," Lola breathlessly said as she felt him enter her. He felt her tighten around his finger and saw how close she was to her limit. Having him back and being back in her little space while she was fucked made her head spin.

"It's ok, baby girl, Daddy, will be gentle. Just say red when you want, little one, Daddy, doesn't want to hurt you," Jake said soothingly before leaning forward and pressing Lola's seat down until she was laying back. Climbing over to her side, he took her panties down and stroked her forehead and hair lovingly as he replaced his finger with the tip of his cock, waiting to see if Lola was still willing.

"Don't just tell Daddy what you think I want to hear," Jake said in a serious tone. Lola just reached for the water bottle that was in the middle console, and Jake felt his cock slide further into Lola as he reached for it and unscrewed the lid.

"Here, baby girl," Jake said, lifting the water to Lola's lips. Drinking, Lola giggled as the water ran down her cheek.

"Thanks, Daddy," Lola said, bucking her hips forward and taking Jake balls deep, surprising him and causing him to moan involuntarily and quickly hump her in excitement.

"Oh god, baby girl," Jake groaned as he felt his balls slap against Lola with each thrust his pushed into her.

"Daddy, you're not allowed to cum," Lola teased, making Jake laugh.

"Oh, little one, it's you that isn't allowed to cum," Jake laughed as both he and Lola came in unison. Panting, Jake pulled out of Lola's tight cunt and squirted another load on top of Lola's heart shaved pussy.

"Damn, baby girl, I didn't think you could be any cuter!" Jake said, wrapping his arms around Lola and feeling her snuggle into his neck.

"I missed you, Daddy," Lola said softly. Jake kissed her forehead and wrapped his arms around her tighter.

"This time, baby girl, Daddy isn't going anywhere," Jake said as they watched the nights sky fill with stars.

Chapter 2

For the next two weeks, Lola looked for a job. She had decided it didn't matter what type of job it was; she just needed one. Successfully gaining employment at a local supermarket, Lola spent her days finding out what the people of her small town used as vices and catching up on the town's gossip.

"Will that be everything?" Lola asked a man who was clearly from out of town. He wore a biker jacket, and the scars on his face made Lola instantly afraid.

"Kane wants to speak with you. Use this," the man said, before handing her a $100 bill for a packet of gum. He had passed her a phone under the note and left without looking back. Taking the tip and phone, Lola quickly placed both in her pocket before her sleazy boss came up behind her.

"Oh, he looks like a nasty piece of work,"

her boss said, squeezing into her station behind her, forcing her to stand facing the next line of customers who had begun to wait for their turn to be served. Turning her head slightly, Lola gave the older man a puzzling look making him laugh.

"Oh, don't mind me, I just want to make sure our newest recruit is alright. You know you can always come to me if you need anything, I can really help you when new positions become available," the older man whispered in Lola's ear, pressing his soft cock into her ass and rubbing himself against her slightly before groping both her ass cheeks with his hands.

"Jack," Lola said, in a soft, slow hiss as she tried to wiggle out of his grasp.

"Yeah, say my name," Jack groaned, before patting her ass predatorily.

"I'll see you later," Jack said, giving Lola's ass a few quick humps before walking away.

"Kane, one of your guys said you wanted to talk to me?" Lola said in her lunch break. She had gone out the back of the supermarket and nervously dialed his number. She knew it by heart. How could she not when they had been together for six years.

"Yeah, I wanted to know if you were settling in properly, heard you had a nice time by the river," Kane said in the smug tone he always used. Lola's eyes grew wide with fear. She had met Kane the first week she had moved to Hollywood. She had been walking down a street late at night when three men had attacked her, taking her handbag and phone before kicking her until she passed out. Kane was the first thing she saw when she opened her eyes again. He had seen what had happened as he ate in a diner and had taken her to his penthouse suite. Lola woke up to ten men standing around her and had begun to cry immediately. Bending down, Kane had shown a side of his heart he was surprised was there as he cared for Lola and never asked for anything in return. He didn't fit the stereotypical biker reputation. He wore the most elegant suits, drove an expensive sports car and only the forearm sleeve dedicated to his gang could give him away that he was, in fact, the kingpin of Hollywood's organized crime. Lola had felt safe with him instantly and had been given her handbag, and phone back along with a significant amount of cash in her wallet she knew could have only come from Kane.

"Kane, I thought we agreed," Lola said, worried he had decided to go back on their deal. Kane just laughed.

"We did agree, I still do, I just want to make sure you remember your part of it," Kane said without a moments pause. He had never been a jealous man; in fact, he had let Lola see many men while she had been under his care. But she wanted more. She wanted to branch off on her own, and that would mean having to have far looser ties to the gang and Kane than she had previously had. He knew it was good for business; he also knew that he had never cared for a woman as much as he cared for Lola.

"Well, I'll be able to start making serious cash, I'm working at the supermarket, the one on Elwood and Fifth, so," Lola said stopping as she saw her boss walk out the back door and eye her greedily.

"Has he tried anything with you?" Kane said, making Lola jump, he could see her from wherever he was.

"I thought we agreed?!" Lola half giggled.

"Please, let me still look after you even though you are all independent and shit," Kane said in a serious voice.

"The cat is in the back, I don't think it's been fed," Lola said before hanging up the phone.

"I didn't know you had a pussy," the older man jeered, standing in the way of the only door out of the small alcove. Lola just shook her head and tried to pass, again being blocked by the man.

"What's puss pusses name then?" He said, grabbing Lola's arm and pulling her into him. She scratched his face which just made him laugh just as Kane jumped the fence and ran at him.

Punching him in the face, the older man let Lola go, and Kane held her tightly, kissing her cheek and glaring at her boss with murder in his eyes.

"Sweetie, you want to take the rest of the day off?" Kane said without looking at her, Lola just nodded and kissed Kane before walking through the door and out of sight. Kane had not dressed in his usual handsome suits and fancy jewelry. He wore combat boots and baggy jeans, a tight black t-shirt which showed his swol, jail made muscles and hadn't bothered to shave in four days.

"Do you like picking on little girls. Does it make you feel like a big man?" Kane asked as he began punching the other man's face. After breaking his jaw, eye socket, and cheekbone, Kane moved onto kicking in his ribs and shattering in his knee cap.

"Don't fucking touch her again," Kane calmly said, casually jumping the fence and out of sight once again.

"What do you mean the cat hasn't been fed?" Kane asked an hour later; he had rung Lola again, this time from a different phone.

"I mean it, from everything I have seen, she's hungry," Lola said.

"That's what I'm asking about, why are you so interested in this cat, she's too big to feed all on your own," Kane replied. Lola just laughed, whenever they spoke about drug runs they always used this code, she had wondered how the police had never caught them before.

"That was not the deal Lola," Kane said, breathing deeply down the phone.

"Are you, are you fucking someone?" Lola asked as she heard Kane's groan and the slap of his balls against something.

"Yeah well, a man's gotta eat," Kane just laughed as he pulled out of the girl he had just emptied his load in.

"Now, the deal was, you go back home and live happily ever after and if you find an open market you tell me, not, you go ahead and try to run it yourself," Kane said taking a beer from the fridge and sitting on the end of the bed of the cheap motel. He hadn't stayed in a place like this for years and had to admit it felt nice getting back to his roots. Kane had come along way from being the son of a whore, a street kid, a punk who used to sell smack under a bridge and run from cops. Now he didn't have to run, he just had to pay them, and whenever they got too greedy, a blue-blooded hero would get the send off a true asset to the city deserves. He didn't have to worry about the politicians either; they were his highest paying clients. Wherever there was somebody they needed to be taken care off, he was their go-to guy. He knew that he was just as expendable as the people he dealt with, but he also knew that after you've fucked enough of their daughters with the videos to prove it, not many senators would try and fuck with you.

"I'm not trying to run it; I'm just saying that I could. Please let me feed this cat, I know you think that only you can do it, but I can too," Lola said, the begging in her voice turning Kane on.

"Fine, give her a little piece of meat and see if she'll purr for you, but back the fuck off if she doesn't, do you understand?" Kane said, waiting for Lola's answer. She thought back to all the lessons she had learned from Kane, how to hustle and hide product, how to smuggle it without anyone even noticing. No-one suspects a woman in the game and she knew that was her greatest advantage.

"Yes, Kane," Lola said before hanging up the phone.

Jake had been around Lola's every day since her return. She hadn't told him about her boss; she hadn't needed too. Kane had taken care of it. She liked being the girl Jake thought she still was, she liked being his baby but always felt nervous when she thought about Kane finding out. Would he think she was weird, she had tried it a few times with him, but he hadn't known what she was wanting, so she had just left it alone. But after laying in Jake's arms again, she knew she couldn't live without it anymore.

"Hi, baby," Jake said, jumping out of his truck and running across the road to where Lola was standing. Lola had decided to wear her hair up tonight in a slicked back pony-tail, and red lipstick, her white body-con dress and red heels making Jake have to clench his fists a couple of times as he fought himself to keep his cock from hardening.

"I thought you'd like it, Daddy, I dressed for you tonight," Lola whispered in his ear as she casually wrapped her arms around his waist and leaned back, pressing her pussy against him.

"Fuck me; you look hot!" Jake gasped holding Lola, getting lost in her big green eyes.

"I could say the same about you, Daddy," Lola said, taking his hand and walking into the cinemas with him. They collected their tickets, paid for popcorn, and made their way to their seats. The cinema was almost empty, with only a few people sitting in the middle as the lights went out and Jake led Lola to a section at the back. She knew that she would be fucked, and her pussy moistening with excitement. Jake took off his jacket and placed it over Lola's lap, moving her, so she was resting up against his muscular torso and cuddling into him.

"Shh, baby girl," Jake whispered as he took out a thick vibrator from his pocket and reached up Lola's dress.

"Naughty girl," Jake teased, feeling that Lola wasn't wearing any panties. She felt Jake flick her with his finger and she spread her thighs for him, trying not to gasp as he began coating the toy with her pussy juices as the movie started. As the commercials played on the big screen, Jake, satisfied that the toy wouldn't hurt Lola, he forced her pussy to take it and shoved it deep inside her. Pulling her close to him to muffle her moans as he turned in on, Jake pinched her nipples through her dress, enjoying how her tits filled his palm.

"Such a good girl for Daddy," Jake said, holding Lola as the film they had long forgotten they were seeing started to play.

"This'll be a long two hours for you, little girl, let Daddy know when you can't take it anymore, and I'll replace it with my cock and finish you off," Jake said, taking out a pacifier and pushing it into Lola's mouth, startling her.

"Don't be naughty for Daddy, or someone might come and see what you're fussy for," Jake said, settling into his seat with Lola horny and moaning by his side.

As the movie played on, Jake let his hand grope at Lola carelessly, only adding to her frustration and as the film neared the end, Lola knew that she couldn't take the teasing any longer.

"Please fuck me, Daddy," Lola said, her desperate begging taking Jake by surprise. He hadn't thought she could be so willing to be taken as she pushed the toy from her cunt and sat her up on his lap.

"You know what to do," Jake whispered in her ear as he pulled his cock from his pants, leaving his full balls under his belt, enjoying the sensation of the pressure. Lola lifted off him slightly as Jake rolled her dress up over her ass before pulling her hips down onto his waiting cock, forcing her to sit on his lap and take him fully, bending her forward, so she was resting her folded arms on the chair in front of her. Pulling her hips down onto his lap more deeply, Jake felt his balls being rubbed by Lola's firm ass cheeks as she ground on him like a stripper. Bouncing her up, he pulled out of her just to force her back down, making her gasp as she was taken from behind. Jake knew the film would end, and knew that he wanted to have his cum filling Lola's cunt before that happened as he sped up his onslaught, taking Lola's throat in one of his hands while holding her down on him with his other as he pounded her aggressively. Cumming deep inside of her, Jake quickly slid a pull-up up Lola's legs and around her waist, rolled her dress back down over her now puffy ass and tied his denim jacket around her waist. Surprised, Lola touched the pull up and wriggled in Jake's arms, unsure of how she felt.

"Be a good girl for Daddy; a little girl always

does what her Daddy tells her," Jake said as the lights of the cinema turned on. He smiled warmly at Lola as he took her hand and enjoyed watching her try to steady herself on her heels as the pull-up spread her thighs.

"Good thing Daddy had a jacket, baby girl, or everyone would see that you are just a little girl pretending to be a grown-up," Jake whispered as he opened his truck door for Lola to climb in. Waiting before she sat down, Jake gently took her wrists and cuffed them to the sides of the passenger seat, surprising Lola again.

"You're not the only one who has a done up truck, baby girl," Jake said, kissing her passionately. Feeling her nipples hardening, Jake knew that he would enjoy what he had planned for her next. Breaking the kiss, he closed the door and walked around to the other side of the truck and begun driving out of town.

"Where are we going, Daddy," Lola asked Jake who just shook his head.

"It's a secret," he replied, pushing a pacifier

past Lola's lips and pressing his fingers against it until she stopped refusing him.

"Good girl," Jake said, patting the top of her head. Lola watched as they drove for another hour, growing sleepy as the tree-lined woods lined each side of the road. Opening her eyes as they drove up a gravel driveway, Jake ran his fingertips through Lola's soft hair as she took in the big red farmhouse they were approaching.

"I bought this property a few years back and have been doing it up slowly," Jake said stopping the car and sitting out the front of the big home with the tall green trees surrounding it as he reached his hand over to Lola's tits and pulled on them until she moaned. Laughing, he got out of the car and walked around to her side, uncuffed her wrists and carried her into the house. Lola snuggled into Jake as he held her and knew that he wouldn't fuck her again tonight. He took her on a tour of the house, showing her the modern, country style kitchen, bathrooms and living room. Walking into an empty room and placing her down on the plush carpet.

"This could be your room if you wanted, little one," Jake said sitting on the floor with Lola who had kicked off her shoes and was trying to take her dress off.

"Here, let Daddy help you," Jake said, pulling her dress off quickly, before taking his t-shirt off and using it to wipe her lipstick off. Watched as Jake's shirt was ruined before her eyes, the same shirt he had bought only days previously. Lola was surprised he would ruin a perfectly good shirt by staining it with lipstick.

"It doesn't matter, baby girl, Daddy has others," Jake said, pulling her into his arms. He had seen Lola like this before, but enjoying how sweet and cute she looked now couldn't compare.

"You are even more beautiful than I remember Lola," Jake whispered into her ear as he cradled her in his arms, making Lola giggle and search for her binky.

"Here it is, little girl. Come on, let's get you bathed and ready for bed," Jake said, standing up and lifting Lola into his arms, before carrying her to the bathroom.

Chapter 3

"Hey, have you heard what happened to Jack?" One of Lola's colleagues asked, rushing into the lunch room the following week. Lola had not heard, however, had a fair idea of what would have happened. Trying to sound surprised, Lola put her salad down and looked at the woman with a curious gaze. The woman looked happy.

"No, what?" Lola asked, watching as the woman sat down and looked around the room, her voice becoming a whisper.

"He got jumped and has been in the hospital for since Friday. Some out of towner jumped him while he was walking home after his shift," the woman said, trying to hide her smirk.

"He tried it on with you too, huh?" Lola asked, the woman suddenly looking like she had been caught out.

"Yeah, I'm happy karma got him," the woman said before walking passed Lola and out of the lunch room. *Karma didn't get him, Kane did* thought Lola as she smiled and went back to eating her salad.

Lola had the closing shift the next day, and she had been waiting for it all week. Deciding to take on extra responsibilities, she had said that she would audit the storage room. Lola had told everyone at the staff meeting that she would have to stay later and was happy when no one offered to help her. She said goodbye to the woman who had told her about Jack's hospital visit and closed the store. This is what she had been waiting for, the perfect time to case the store to see how she would bring the shipment in and get the money out. Kane had told her to be careful, that she would need three routes if she were to go undetected. Walking into the storage room, Lola saw the shelves of chemicals, brooms, and sponges, rags, and all the junk that was stored in there because everyone was too lazy to put it in the correct place. Knowing that she would have to clean the room and have some data to justify the long time she would be spending in there, Lola took photos of the room and spent them to the man replacing Jack. She also sent the images to Kane, who just sent her a laughing smiley in response.

After three hours, the shelves were cleaned, the chemicals and cleaning products sorted, and the remaining junk had either been thrown in the trash or placed in the correct place. Lola had found a hole behind one of the tiles that could be easily reached and concealed and took a photo of it and sent it to Kane as well, writing a message at how if she were the boss she would seal it up. He replied by saying, *if only you were in charge*, and Lola put her phone back in her pocket after she had baited the hole in the wall. She had placed the change from the $100 note one of Kane's men had given her in the wall and knew that she would now have to monitor the potential drop spot for the next two months. Lola also knew that she would have to watch the shifts for who was working when to see if firstly, anyone knew the hole was there, secondly, if anyone was even looking and thirdly if it was a safe place to hide the stash.

Lola was thinking about Kane when Jake messaged, asking if she was free and if she wanted to go for afternoon coffee. A smile spreading across her face instantly, Lola replied with a time and location.

"You're early," she said, as she entered the artsy café causing Jake to laugh.

"So are you!" He exclaimed, standing up and holding her in a hug. Lola looked down to the object on the table and couldn't help her laugh from escaping.

"You still have this?" She asked, sitting down and opening the photo album they had made on Lola's 20th birthday.

"How could I get rid of it, you looked so cute, especially in all these photos where you refused to smile," Jake said pointing to the photos highlighting the emo phase Lola had fully embraced.

"How did you find me cute?! I look terrifying," Lola said, slowly turning the pages and feeling all the memories flood back to her. The time they had gone bowling and been kicked out for pushing too many balls down the alley. The time they had written off Jake's Father's car when they went drifting and had crashed into a tree. They both knew they were lucky to escape that one.

"Hey, Jake!" Lola said, looking at the photo of her in a diaper that he had stuck to the last page. Jake just laughed.

"Sorry I hadn't realized it was in there, but look how cute, don't you miss those days," Jake teased, causing Lola to roll her eyes.

"No, not really," Lola said, crossing her arms and sitting back in the chair as the waitress took their order. Jake watched as Lola bit her bottom lip and waited for the waitress to leave their table with the order of two black coffees.

"I like this more," Lola finally said, looking down at the album once more.

"How's work?" Jake asked, as their coffee came quickly to their table. Lola just laughed and looked out the window. She wished she could tell Jake of all her plans, how she was getting her first shipment and that her cut was 30% of the profits, and how she had successfully hoodwinked the town. She wondered how proud of his baby girl; he would be if he knew who she had become. She wondered how proud of herself she was.

"Good, hey, can we not talk about it. I kinda just want to sit here," Lola asked, frowning and trying to feel comfortable. Jake sipped his coffee and looked at her over the top of his cup, trying to figure her out before he spoke again.

"I know what you need, come with me," Jake said, standing up and holding out his hand to Lola.

"It's not your dick," Lola said, more annoyed than she wished she was.

"I am aware," Jake replied, helping her put

on her coat and walking her out of the café.

"Are you taking me home, Daddy," Lola said, as she softened the minute she was sitting in his truck, watching as Jake covered her in her old fluffy blankie.

"Yeah, baby girl. I think it's time you let Daddy really take care of you," Jake said, driving them to his farmhouse.

"I've made a few adjustments; I think you'll love it, baby," he said as they pulled into the newly built driveway. Lola snuggled into the blankie as Jake unbuckled her seatbelt, not wanting the blankie to be taken away.

"You don't have to worry, Daddy's got you," Jake said, kissing Lola's cheek and lifting her out of the rig.

"Come on, it's late," Jake said, taking Lola inside and straight to the bathroom. He ran her a warm bath filled with bubbles and watched as she melted into her little headspace.

"There's my little one," Jake said, as Lola began to draw on the side of the bath with the bath crayons he had bought for her.

"Let Daddy, wash your hair baby girl," Jake said, taking a jug and pouring water over Lola's head, careful not to get water in her eyes. Taking the shampoo and conditioner that Lola had told him was her favorite, he gently made her clean.

"Daddy," Lola said, before slipping under the water to wash the final soap from her body and hair.

"I love you," Lola said, coming back to the surface, surprised that the words had escaped her lips. She had planned to say thank you and blushed as the words she had kept so close to her heart for so long were now shared. Jake smiled, his eyes softening and his heart melting. Running his hand over Lola's wet hair, and bending down to kiss her forehead, he winked at her.

"I love you too, baby girl," he replied, taking a dry towel and lifting Lola from the bath, and drying her off. Taking her hand, Jake led her to the previously empty nursery.

"I told you I had made some changes," Jake

said, opening the door and taking the towel from Lola. He had hired an out of town interior designer who specialized in the DDlg kink to design the room. After giving her specifics about the kind of little things Lola liked, he was sure she would love how the room turned out. Stunned, Lola explored the room, feeling overwhelmed and excited all at the same time.

"What do you think, baby girl, if you hate it, we can change it," Jake asked as he watched Lola explore. Lola looked over the mounted walls shelving a collection of stuffies, the crib with the softest, fluffiest blankies she had ever felt and the wall length window where a wide, pink, soft fabric booth was placed. She saw the feature wall with built-in niches that she could easily make forts in and turned around to look at Jake in astonishment.

"You did this all for me, Daddy?" Lola asked, her eyes still gazing around the room in wonder. Jake popped Lola's pink binky into her mouth before answering.

"Yes, little one. Now come on, I need to get

you dressed before you catch a cold," Jake said, taking Lola and laying her down on the booth. She lay down, and Jake watched as she looked out the window and into the woods of his property.

"The windows are tinted so heavily from the outside that you can see out, but even with the lights on at night, no one can see it," he explained.

"Lift up for Daddy," Jake said, watching as Lola lifted her bottom up as he slid a thick puffy diaper under her.

"I don't want that one, Daddy," Lola squirmed, stopping when Jake gently but firmly gripped her thighs.

"Don't be a bad girl for Daddy, or I'll take my belt off and use it to make that little bottom red and sore," he said in a stern voice that made Lola stop fussing and accept the diaper Jake had chosen for her. Satisfied, he let her thighs go, before powdering her and securing the diaper in place.

"Little girl's need diapers for beddies, baby girl," Jake said, taking a navy blue diaper cover and dressing Lola in it. Jake liked that the cover was one size too small, making the diaper push into Lola's pussy, making her squirm as he pulled it up and over her diaper.

"Shh, little one," Jake said, pulling a white t-shirt over Lola's head and breasts, shaking her body slightly after he had dressed her.

"Cute little girl, time for your bottle," Jake said, lifting Lola up and into his arms. He wasn't as broad or muscular as Kane. However, Lola suspected Jake was stronger. His strength seemed to come from a protective place, rather than brute force. Jake lay Lola down on the couch and placed the pillows around her gently before going into the kitchen and making her a protein shake in her bottle.

"Daddy wants you nice and full my little one; I can't have my baby girl hungry can I?" Jake called from the kitchen. Lola just sucked her binky and closed her eyes as she snuggled into the blankies, being taken by surprise when she felt the nipple of the bottle against her lips. Jake skilfully pushed the bottle into her mouth while taking out the pacifier and moved Lola into his arms as he fed her, rocking her slowly and watching as her tummy became full.

Chapter 4

When Lola woke up the next morning, she knew where she was with immediate clarity. As she turned in Jake's arms, sunlight streamed through the window, and she nudged him until he was awake. Feeling between her thighs, Jake smirked.

"Some things haven't changed," he said stretching and looked at Lola expectantly.

"But I don't wanna, Daddy," Lola whined, hoping that she wouldn't have to wet her diaper. Jake just wrapped his arms around her and held her tight.

"I know you don't, baby girl, but that doesn't mean you aren't going to," Jake whispered in her ear as he patted her thickly padded bottom. He moved, so his large thigh was spreading her and began to bounce her up and down, watching as Lola giggled and tried to push away from him.

"You can't escape, Daddy, little one. Daddy makes all the rules, and you will have to wet that diaper before I let you out of it," Jake teased. Lola just whimpered as she knew that she truly wouldn't get away without wetting herself. She just stubbornly shook her head and pouted, causing Jake to laugh and push her off him.

"It doesn't worry me; if I had my way, you'd be diaper 24/7. Daddy can wait, but I don't know how much longer you can," Jake said, seeing Lola have to fight herself not to wet her diaper. Jake got out of bed and took Lola to the nursery.

"What about breakfast, Daddy?" Lola asked as he took one of her wrists and cuffed it to a chain that was secured to a wall.

"I'm going to go make it, but I want you to stay here," Jake said, kissing Lola on the top of her head before walking out. Lola pulled on the long chain she had been connected to before realizing that she could still move freely around the room and reached up for the stuffies that were sitting on the shelves. After collecting all of them, she made her way to one of the niches in the wall and began playing, just as Jake came back.

"Look what Daddy has for you," Jake said, holding a purple plastic plate with a dino pancake on it. Lola excitedly clapped her hands and crawled to Jake who let her sit in his lap as he fed her. Waiting until she was finished, Jake went back to the kitchen to get her bottle. Filling it with water, he smirked knowing that she would be wetting her diaper sooner rather than later

"Drink it up for Daddy," Jake said, holding Lola's mouth open as he forced the bottle into her mouth.

"Daddy's fussy girl," Jake said, rubbing her pussy as she drank. Lola knew it was coming; she pouted as she wet her diaper, blushing as Jake smirked at her, making her stay humiliated, so she remembered who was in charge. He stayed pushing the bottle into her mouth and making her drink until the whole bottle was empty before softening his gaze again.

"Next time, just do what Daddy says, little

girl," Jake said, lifting her up and taking her to the bathroom. He undressed her and took her diaper off, running a shower for her, their old trigger to highlight the end of their play. Jake watched as Lola transformed back into the smart-mouthed, beautiful woman he loved so dearly and smiled as she opened the door and pulled him into the shower with her.

"You've got me all wet. I could have had my phone in my pocket," Jake laughed, as Lola began undressing him.

"Well, that would have sucked," she replied, feeling relaxed for the first time in weeks. Jake watched as she slowly took off his shirt and pants, his cock boldly bobbing out in front of him.

"Where do you want to stick it, Daddy," Lola teased, taking the shower head off the wall and placing it between her thighs, the pressure of the water hitting her clit making her moan instantly. Jake didn't speak; he just watched as Lola got herself off in front of him. Reaching out, he groped her tits, pulling on her nipples and biting them before taking his long cock in his hand and jerking himself. Turning Lola around and slapping his dick between her ass cheeks, Jake pressed the tip between her cheeks and slid it up and down, enjoying her clenching them together as she felt him trying to enter her.

"Are you playing hard to fuck, baby girl, do you want Daddy to show you how bad girls get fucked," Jake whispered in her ear, causing her to push her ass out and begin twerking on his cock.

"That's it, Daddy's little slut," Jake said, slapping her ass until both cheeks were red. Jake grabbed both Lola's hips in his hands and guided his cock into her, pushing the shower head out of the way as he claimed her.

"I'm going to make you my little cock puppet baby girl, by the time I'm done with you, you won't want to move without my huge snake up you," Jake said, fish-hooking Lola's mouth as he began pounding into her. Lola just moaned as she was taken, Jake pushing her onto the floor of the shower and using her ass and shoulders as support as he speared her time and time again. Lola could feel her abs being destroyed but stayed pinned to the ground as Jake finished hard, squirting deep inside of her, making her wonder how one man could have so much cum. Pulling out of her, Jake picked Lola up in his arms and cradled her, taking the shower head and cleaning her as best he could.

"You'll need another diaper little one, I can't have your pussy leaking into your panties," Jake said with a kind smile. He took Lola back to the nursery, diapered her again and this time, dressed her in a fluffy pink onesie with bunny ears attached to the hood.

Lola had gone to work the next day as though she hadn't just been a little girl for the last two days and smirked to herself when people asked how her weekend was.

"Oh, fine thanks," Lola replied to the third person who had asked the mundane question. As she approached the storage room, she saw two familiar faces and left the door unlocked as she entered the small space. Walking to the end of the room before turning around, she saw one of the men lock the door and stand in front of it.

"I was wondering when you two would show up. You can tell Kane that the cat has been fed I'm just waiting for her to eat," Lola said. The two men looked at each other and nodded their heads at her.

"Kane sent us here to make sure, just keep doing what you are doing, does he know you're fucking that guy?" one of the men asked. Lola just rolled her eyes.

"I was never Kane's. So yes, he knows," Lola spat back, angry that her cunt had always been everyone's top priority. Both men just snorted before walking to leave the room.

"It'll be tonight. Come to this address," the man who had done all the talking instructed. Lola looked at the address before putting the piece of paper in her pocket and watching both men leave.

It was 9 O'clock when Lola arrived at the location, and she was immediately surprised.

"I wasn't expecting to see you here," Lola said, walking over to Kane. He opened his arms to her and held her tenderly, his arms snaking their way under the opening of her oversized, stylish jacket and placing the package of drugs down the back of her pants. Kane leaned back and looked at Lola; he could see something was different with her tonight, and it made him unsettled.

"What's going on with you?" He asked, letting Lola go. She stepped back and saw Kane's muscle back-up step forward.

"Nothing, what's going on with you?" Lola scoffed back, insulted that he would question her loyalty.

"If I fuck this, it hurts me a lot more than you. If it's proof you want, here," Lola said, starting to take off her clothes. Kane knew that the look on her face meant that she was hurt her, but he let her prove her innocence.

"Snitches get ditches; everyone knows that.

I can't believe you think I'd do you like that," Lola said, as she took off her bra and threw it in his face.

"Lola, I just had to be sure," Kane said, softer than he had expected he would. Shifting uncomfortably as he saw Lola's toned body, naked in front of him, he signaled for his crew to disappear from sight.

"I just have to be sure, baby," Kane said, offering Lola her clothes back. Lola took them, held them in her hand for a moment before throwing them done on the ground again.

"Do you miss me?" Lola asked, reaching out to grab Kane's hardening bulge in his pants. He was bigger than Jake, and Lola had always had to cum several times before she could fit him inside of her. As Kane reached between her thighs, he fingered her, sighing as he felt her familiar wetness. Sliding his finger in, he was surprised that she was so open and willing to be taken.

"You've had a dick in you haven't you," he said, sliding another finger inside of Lola making her reach for his forearm to steady herself.

"That's the moaning girl I know," Kane said. He wiggled his fingers, happy Lola's pussy started dribbling juices instantly.

"Such a beautiful slut. Get over here," Kane said, grabbing Lola by her hair and pushing her onto the back of his bike.

"New?" Lola asked as he took his fingers out of her wet pussy and shoved them in her mouth.

"Shut up bitch, yeah it's new, and I've been waiting for your pretty little cunt to christen it," Kane said, pushing his pants down and coating his cock in Lola's juices before sliding his rock hard dick into her until she gasped.

"Take all this dick," Kane growled as he pulled out of her and pushed back in, pounding her, making her tits shake in time with his forceful thrusts.

"Cum for, Daddy," Kane said, holding himself inside of her as his orgasm built. He knew he wanted to cream her hard and deep, but as he heard a car approaching, he aggressively pounded her again, cumming quickly and pulling his still hard cock from her sopping cunt.

"Make sure they get delivered," Kane said before pushing her off the bike, pulling his pants back up and driving away. Lola just rolled her eyes, and reached for her clothes, quickly dressing and walking to her truck, but stopped when she saw who was coming in the car.

"Hey, what are you doing all the way out here?" Jake asked, his headlights shining brightly.

"Just felt like looking at the stars," Lola calmly answered, she could feel her panties getting wetter and wetter as Kane's cum dripped from her pussy.

"On my property?" Jake questioned. He had mischief in his voice, but Lola was shocked. She knew Jake's house was close but had no idea the property was so large.

"I actually didn't know it was your property. I guess that's why you came to investigate," Lola replied. It was starting to rain, and a silence fell between the two of them.

"You could always come inside, and out of the rain if you'd like, I've got hot chocolate on the stove, and the fire is burning?" Jake said, smiling at Lola like he knew she would say yes.

"Only if I can have a shower first, I've had a really long day and just want to wash it all off," she replied, impressed with herself that she had found a way to get out of her ruined clothes without Jake ever finding out. She had planned to wet her panties with water from the shower she was about to have and pretend that she had accidentally flung them in the shower and smiled sweetly to him.

"Deal, come on, let's get you dry. I have a cup of hot chocolate back at mine with your name on it in sparkly pink writing. Maybe if you are a good girl you'll get some marshmallows to go with it as well," Jake said, sitting back in his car and waiting for Lola to follow him in her truck. What both of them were wilding unaware of was that Kane had been watching the whole thing from just behind the tree line. *So you're the guy who's fucking my bitch*, Kane thought. He thought for another moment before turning his bike back on. *I'll see you later,* Kane thought, driving off in the other direction.

Chapter 5

Lola stayed the night at Jake's and waking up before him in the early hours of the morning, she quietly got out of bed and tip-toed through the living room and into the kitchen. Making a cup of coffee, Lola pulled her jacket tightly around her wanting to be warmer. She had kept the drugs in her truck, not wanting Jake to find them, not wanting him to find out who she had willingly become.

"Hi," Jake said, startling Lola and making her spill her coffee on the floor.

"Oh shit, sorry," Lola said, putting her cup down and running to find something to clean it up. Jake just laughed as he chased after her and grabbed her arm.

"It doesn't matter," he said, reaching into the cupboard and taking down the paper towels.

Walking over to the mess on the floor, Jake bent down to casually clean it up.

"Do you want to tell me what you were doing out there last night?" Jake said, seeing the look in Lola's eyes and knowing that he was onto something.

"Don't try to lie to me, baby girl, Daddy knows you weren't trying to look at stars," Jake said, handing Lola back her coffee cup. Lola looked down into her half-empty mug and bit her bottom lip. *Fuck*, she thought, submitting to Jake's desire to know the truth, and looking back up at his hopeful eyes.

"I don't want to lose this. If I tell you, it'll be gone," Lola said honestly. Jake just nodded his head.

"Well, nothing has torn us apart yet, so, tell me and let's see what we can do about it," Jake said with an expression Lola couldn't pick.

"I've started bringing drugs into the town for the Venom Motorcycle Club. Last night I was picking up my first shipment. It'll be dispersed tomorrow," Lola said in one long breath. Jake just smirked and went to his office and came back with the package that Lola was sure was still in her truck.

"Hey," Lola said, reaching for the product.

"No, don't. Why are you doing this?" Jake asked, holding the drugs out of reach.

"Because it's easy money, Jake," Lola said, calling him by his name, causing him to raise an eyebrow.

"Well, Lola, I can't let you get any further than you are already in," Jake replied, emphasizing her name in response. Lola just rolled her eyes and sighed before going to sit down on Jake's couch.

"I used to date, super casually, the king of Hollywood, and well, he gave me the go-ahead to branch out and try the market here," Lola began explaining.

"I guess you can't just, give them back, can you?" Jake asked, making Lola laugh.

"No, that's not how this works," Lola replied.

"Look, give me them back. I got myself into this, and to be fair; I don't want out. Do you know how much money I can make, hell, you've got a million dollar baby girl right here," Lola said, catching the package Jake gently threw at her.

"Lola, I think you should go," Jake said, feeling his heartbreak. Lola just nodded, turning to speak but being cut off.

"You don't have to worry. I'm not going to tell anyone. I told you I'd always look after you, and that's what I intend to do. But I have to look after me as well, and that means that until, or if you ever, give it up, we can't have this," Jake said, sadly opening his front door and watching as Lola picked up her things and walked out the door.

Lola delivered the package to the allocated place in the wall and came back three weeks later to see her cut of the profits along with the next load. She had made $50,000 in two months but was disappointed that all her wildest dreams were coming true, and yet the only thing she truly wanted seemed to be out of reach. Kane had noticed it too and had decided to take it upon himself to try and sort out what was bothering Lola.

"You don't need to speak with Jake, Kane. He is clean, Jake isn't like us," Lola said to him over the champaign breakfast they were sharing on his yacht. The simple life had become too triggering, and he had returned to his former luxury.

"If he can't see that you having everything you want isn't a good thing, then maybe I should knock some sense into the boy," Kane said, dismissing the three women who entered from the downstairs bedroom.

"Really?" Lola laughed, watching Kane shrug his shoulders.

"It's cold out here at night," he said, pretending to plead his case. Lola looked out over the ocean and saw birds ducking for fish and kids fishing from the pier.

"What does he give you that I can't," Kane

asked softly, taking Lola by surprise.

"You called me Daddy all the time. I looked after you and stuff like that," he added, clicking his fingers for the table to be cleared.

"I know. But it's not like that. You are lovely, but you're not a Daddy Daddy. You're a Daddy to a hoe, not a baby, there's a difference," Lola tried to explain. Kane just thought deeply before speaking again.

"I love you, Lola. I love you so much that it fucking kills me. And all I want to do is kill this motherfucker who isn't being your Daddy, so this is what we are going to do. You're going to step down," Kane said, pounding his fist down on the table.

"You're fired," he said laughing and emptied his warm champaign over the side of the boat.

"Really?!" Lola questioned happily. Kane just laughed harder before turning around.

"No! You need to get the fuck over this Josh, Jake, Jay, whatever his name is and remember who you're fucking loyal to. You said you wanted in;

this isn't a fucking merry-go-round that you can just jump on and off as it fucking suits. I swear if you weren't so beautiful, I'd slap the stupid of out you. Now get the fuck out of my face and go do your bloody job," Kane growled, scaring Lola who stood up and walked down the stairs, past Kane's bitches and out onto the pier. The kids suddenly grabbed their buckets and ran to the shore and Lola closed her eyes, knowing what was coming next.

"Lola," one of Kane's men said, sadness escaping his voice. Lola slowly turned around, a tear escaping her eye.

"I'm sorry," the man said before punching her square in her face, kicking her stomach and stomping on her legs as instructed by Kane who let him hit her four more times.

"That'll do," Kane called from the boat before walking back inside, his man following and leaving Lola to lay injured on the wooden planks of the pier.

Lola stayed laying on the pier as she drifted in and out of consciousness until it was well into the night. As she opened her eyes, managing to keep them open as she slowly lifted herself onto her elbows, she noticed the yacht had long gone, as were the cars in the parking lot. *Fuck*, Lola thought once again as she began to stagger to where she had left her truck. Sliding into the driver's seat, Lola locked the doors and cried into her hands. It was dark, cold, and lonely as Lola pressed on the ignition and slowly drove herself home. She thought about Jake, how it would have felt like heaven to be able to drive back to him once more. She thought about Kane and how naïve she had been to think she could get out just like that. *What was I thinking?!* Lola angrily thought to herself as she looked at her beat up reflection in the rear vision mirror.

"Not so pretty now," Lola said out loud as she turned into the apartment she had recently begun renting. Slowly taking off her clothes, Lola walked to the medicine box and popped two pain killers and lay down on the couch before flicking through her phone and seeing Jake had sent her a message.

Hey baby, I think we should talk. I think I've got a solution to your problem.

"Would have been useful a couple of hours ago," Lola muttered as she rang his number.

"Hey, did you get my message?" Jake said, picking up the phone on the first dial. *He has clearly been waiting,* Lola thought, a smile escaping her lips as she tried not to sound like she had just been throttled.

"Yeah, that's why I'm calling," Lola replied, closing her eyes as her head started pounding again.

"Ok, it'll probably be better if we do this in person. Can I come over?" Jake asked, excitedly.

"No, now is not really a good time," Lola replied, hoping that Jake wouldn't need to be told twice.

"Oh, ok, well, when are you free?" Jake asked, waiting silently. Lola felt the tears roll down her cheeks hearing the warmth and love in his voice and wished that she had known what was still waiting for her back in this town before she had sold her soul to Kane.

"Baby?" Jake said interrupting Lola's thoughts.

"Yeah, sorry, um I'm off work tomorrow, come around then. At like 10 in the morning?" Lola asked.

"See you then," Jake replied, happy he had a chance to help her.

Chapter 6

"Baby, what the hell happened to you?!" Jake exclaimed upon seeing Lola's face the next morning. She just tried to smile, but the cut on her lip split and started bleeding. It wasn't the first time this had happened, so she reached into her pocket for her tissue.

"Here, let me look after you, little one," Jake said, rushing into the apartment and going into the bathroom. He wet a washcloth, noticing the significant amount of blood that stained the basin before he left the room. Bringing the washcloth back to Lola, he gently held it to her lip and kissed her forehead lovingly.

"It looks a lot worse than it is," Lola tried to say, trying to believe the lie she was speaking. Jake looked at her dramatically before clearing his throat and frowning at her.

"Who did this to you?" He asked, already knowing the answer.

"After I let here, I went to speak with Kane. I told him I wanted out. I'm not getting out," Lola said, looking down.

"Why did you say you wanted out?" Jake questioned, cupping Lola's face gently in his.

"Because I want you," Lola said softly, as she melted into Jake's touch.

"I always knew you could take a punishment, but I had no idea how strong you were, little one. I think maybe, Daddy might need to keep taking care of you," Jake said, feeling the all too familiar protective love he had for Lola flow through his veins.

"But you said," Lola tried to say but was cut off by Jake's thumb on her lips.

"I know what I said. I was wrong. Daddy can be wrong sometimes, little one," Jake said, opening his arms to Lola and holding her close.

"Come on, let me get you into something more comfortable," Jake said, holding out his hand

and standing Lola up.

He walked her to the main bedroom and gently placed her down on the bed. Slowly taking off her baggy jeans, panties, and an oversized sweater, he saw the extent of her bruising. Her ribs were tender and bruised; her thighs looked as though someone had stepped on them repeatedly. Jake felt a rage begin to boil within him, but he knew that right now Lola needed his love, not his anger.

"Shh, it's alright, baby girl, Daddy is here now," Jake said lovingly. He diapered Lola and dressed her in a duck print onesie. He made a nest out of blankets and pillows before turning on a movie.

"Just stay here while Daddy makes some lunch, ok princess?" Jake said before disappearing into the kitchen.

Lola stayed snuggled up in her blanket nest for the rest of the day, happy that Jake didn't want to talk, he just held her, fed her a bottle and stroked her hair as she sucked on her binky.

"Do you want me to go, little one? Or can I

make us some dinner?" Jake asked as their fourth movie ended. Lola snuggled into him and looked up at him before speaking.

"Can you please stay?" She asked Jake, who smiled and nodded his head.

"I think I should it would seem that you get yourself in trouble when I'm not around," Jake laughed, as he went to investigate what dinner options they had.

Coming back with an oven made pizza, Jake cut Lola's into small pieces as another movie played.

"Baby, I know you've only just moved in here, but I think you should move in with me," Jake said, making Lola's eyes go wide. She had thought that tonight he was just being kind, she hadn't thought that he would want her back in his life.

"Really?" Lola asked in her little voice. She turned in his arms to look at him in the eye.

"Even though I look so yuck?" She added, her self-esteem low now that she had a bruised face.

"You are beautiful, baby girl. And Daddy

loves you very much," Jake said, pausing before he said he loved her. He couldn't deny it, even with her injured body, the gang they would have to manage somehow, he knew he still wanted her.

"I love you too, Daddy," Lola replied, shifting in his arms to snuggle closer to him.

"Well isn't this just perfect," a voice boomed over their heads, sending fear into both their hearts.

"Kane!?" Lola said, ripping herself out of her little space. The usual back up Kane had was nowhere in sight, and he had picked the lock on the door to get in. Kane took out his phone and started taking photos of Lola.

"I wasn't sure what it was about this guy that you liked so much, but now I get it," Kane said, sitting down on a chair opposite to where Lola and Jake where.

"Oh, don't worry about the photos, I'll just print them up and put them around town if you try any of your bullshit again," Kane said, looking at Lola up and down.

"You must be Kane," Jake said, standing up to shake his hand. Kane was amused and played along standing up as well and greeting Jake.

"Oh, so she's told you about me," Kane said, looking Lola aggressively in the eye. Before Lola could speak, Jake answered the man who monstered him.

"Yes, she said you two used to date, back when she was living in Hollywood. She didn't tell me you rode bikes though, that's a cool jacket," Jake said, trying to sound innocent of his knowledge of who Kane was.

"Yeah I ride, I rode that bitch a couple of hundred times. Did she tell you that?" Kane said, trying to bait Jake into a fight.

"Oh, yeah, we all have our pasts don't we," Jake replied, refusing to take the bait. Kane just eyed him, wanting to see if there was any challenge in Jake before getting up from the chair.

"Well, you two have fun now, fuck her in her ass, she loves it," Kane said before leaving out the front door, not bothering to close it. Jake, who had been clenching his calves during the entire encounter, relaxed and walked out behind Kane and closed the door. Walking back into the living room, he looked at Lola, and she stared blankly back at him.

"Daddy, I am so sorry," Lola said, tears breaking from her eyes. She looked fearfully at Jake, worried he would be mad at her.

"You don't need to be afraid of me. I won't ever hurt you, even if I get angry, baby girl. Come here, let Daddy hold you," Jake said, reaching for Lola's pacifier and opening his arms to her. She quickly crawled to him, opened her mouth for her binky and let Jake position her where he wanted before turning the movie back on.

"Baby girl, you're moving in with me, and that's final," Jake said, sitting back down and holding onto Lola as though his life depended on it.

"Come on, let's get you settled again, little one," Jake said, lifting her up into his arms and carrying her to the bedroom. Jake lay her down on her bed and began to undress her. Starting with her the clips of her onesie and pulling it from her body. He took her diaper off next and watched as she wriggled on the bed, before placing her hand on her pussy, playing in front of him.

"Naughty girl, you know, Daddy can just," Jake said, pulling his cock out and pressing it against Lola's wetness, making it grow hard as he toyed with her.

"Come on, bend down and touch your toes for Daddy," Jake said, pulling Lola's arm up and standing her up. Obediently, Lola reached for her ankles as Jake pressed his soft sack against her, his cock resting along her ass crack.

"So easy," Jake said, sliding his now rock hard cock inside Lola's cunt, groaning as he took her balls deep. Holding both her hips, he fucked her roughly, pumping in and out as he got off quickly, wanting to use her as a cum dumpster for a moment. Squirting into her, Jake smiled as he leaned back and let his orgasm finish inside of Lola who had stayed quietly holding her ankles while he enjoyed her.

"Now, where was I," Jake said, pulling out of her and going back to dressing her. He wiped her pussy down with a wet wipe before powdering her and fastening the tabs of her night diaper around her waist. He took a pacifier and placed it in her mouth, enjoying the sucking sounds she made while he rolled on her thigh high black fluffy socks on her, next came her white diaper cover and fuzzy pink sweater which he had bought her last week. Although her tits were a generous handful, this sweater made her look particularly busty, and Jake liked how ripe and ready she looked to be taken.

Chapter 7

Jake was on the phone to the best fence building company in town the next week. He had thought that a fence going around the property would look ugly, but after the encounter, he and Lola had with Kane the previous night, he had reconsidered. It was due to take three weeks, and Jake had moved some of his things in with Lola while the construction crew made the 8ft stone wall with built-in electric wiring for added security. He had also arranged for multiple security cameras to be placed throughout the property, with sensors and warning triggers to be activated straight to his phone and the houses mainframe.

"Dogs, we should also get dogs," Jake said over breakfast. Lola just laughed.

"I think the luxurious prison you're creating will be safe enough, Daddy," Lola said, drinking from her sippy cup.

"You are probably right, but let's get dogs anyway," Jake said, flicking through the pounds adoption website.

"Look, these look like they could be alright. They need an active lifestyle and lots of space to run and explore. Plus they are huge. Says they have basic skills but are intelligent and easily trained," Jake said, reading out the description of the dogs. Lola stood up and walked to where Jake was sitting. Pushing him back, wanting to sit on his lap, Lola wrigged as she positioned herself on Jake comfortably before looking at the dogs he had selected.

"They look a bit scary, Daddy," Lola said, unsure of his selection.

"That's the point. I want two dogs who get along with us but scare everyone else. We should go to have a look today," Jake said, kissing Lola's face. It had healed quickly, and Jake had enjoyed testing her recovery with his cock. He had steadily increased the intensity in which he fucked her for the last week, giving it to her balls deep the previous night and deciding she was ready to taken again.

"Daddy wants to see what you've got on under there," Jake whispered in Lola's ear, licking her earlobe as his hands snaked their way to her thighs, forcing them to be spread open. He liked that she hadn't worn any panties, just her oversized bed shirt that he was already tugging off her. Pulling her pussy lips back, he slid a finger from each hand into her cunt and stretched her.

"Such a pretty girl," Jake said, reaching into his jean pocket and pulling out a bunny butt plug.

"Make it wet for Daddy," Jake said, pushing the plug into Lola's mouth and forcing her to suck it. Gagging on it, Lola felt Jake's cock hardening under her and knew that she was going to be used to his satisfaction today.

"Good girl," Jake moaned, as Lola began to grind on top of him, reaching back to spread her ass cheeks for him and twerk on his rod. Jake let Lola perform for him, watching how her ass jiggled with each twerk, feeling how her pussy juices made his pants wet, but mostly just enjoying how it felt to want to bury his cock inside of her but make himself wait.

"Daddy's got a juicy treat for you, little one," Jake said, taking the plug from Lola's lips and entering her ass as her cheeks clapped together. Jake stood up, pushing Lola to her knees and unzipped his jeans. He watched as his pre-cum sprayed onto Lola's face, her mouth open and her tongue as she stuck it out like he had trained her to do. Bending his knees slightly, he slid his hard, heavy meat into her waiting mouth and pushed down her throat until she was gagging around his balls.

"You love a bit of sausage for breakfast don't you," Jake said, watching as Lola's lips pouted around his cock as he slowly pulled out of her, only to ram himself back in, this time holding her head to him as she tried to free herself from the invading rod.

"No, you'll take it, just like the pretty little

slut you are," Jake said, loving while watching Lola's eyes water. Pulling out and watching Lola gasp, Jake walked behind her and bent her forward.

"Show Daddy your pretty princess pussy, baby girl," Jake said, reaching under Lola and placing his hand on the soft part of her abs as he positioned his cock halfway in her pussy.

"Daddy wants to feel how your little tummy pushes out when my fat cock splits you open," Jake whispered while slowly filling Lola as she moaned and dipped her head in submission.

"Yeah, you'll take it how Daddy wants, won't you, baby girl," Jake said, holding her hips and swaying against her while keeping his cock buried up her cunt. Lola knew he didn't want to hear her response by the way he pushed a pacifier in her mouth as he fucked her. Pounding her from behind, Lola made little moans as each time Jake pushed against her ass, she was jerked forward, and pulled back as he pulled out.

"Such a cute girl," Jake said, turning Lola

around and laying her on her back. He lifted her legs, and she held them in place as she presented her exposed, dripping cunt to him. Jake smiled in delight as he saw the cream he just filled her with ooze from her soft pink parts before he placed both hands on the floor either side of her and let his hips drop down forcefully.

"Oh, Daddy is lucky to have such a beautiful little girl like you to play with," Jake said, pumping her harder and faster as he felt his cock explode inside Lola's warm, wet, hole. Pulling out of her and jerking his cock over her, Jake placed one foot on her tummy and pinned her to the floor as he jerked his cock hard until cum spilled down onto her.

"Who is Daddy's little cum whore?" Jake said, bending down to take the pacifier from Lola's lips.

"I am, Daddy," Lola said, as Jake straddled her tits and begun sliding his cum coated cock between her tits. Content with just playing, Jake slapped her tits with his cock, rubbing her nipples with it, making them wet and hard. He got up and lifted her into his arms before carrying her to the bedroom. Placing her down on the bed, he took out ankle and wrist cuffs and secured her in a hogtie, leaving her neck unrestrained.

"One more time, baby girl," Jake said, loving as he stroked her hair. Kissing her forehead before he went behind her once again, Jake placed a pillow under Lola's tummy before slapping her ass with both hands, grabbing handfuls of her soft flesh and shaking it in his hands.

"Yeah, Daddy's dirty girl. Come on, shake that ass for Daddy," Jake said, standing back and watching how Lola skilfully twerked against her restraints, her bunny butt plug bouncing up and down and the cum Jake had pumped her full of dribbling out of her gash.

"Damn girl," Jake said, suddenly gripping her thighs and pulling her onto his pulsing cock.

"Daddy's home," Jake said as he picked her up and turned her over so that she was forced to take him over and over as he bounced her on top of him. Trying to wriggle away, Jake slapped her tits, pinching her nipples and holding her down on him firmer.

"Where do you think you are going?" He growled as he dumped his load in her once again.

"Is it too much? Do you need Daddy to go easy on you?" Jake mocked, pushing her off him and onto the bed, watching as his cock slipped from her used cunt. He uncuffed her wrists and ankles and picked her up, cradling her in his arms as he carried her to the shower.

"Lola, are you alright?" Jake said as he saw the red marks that were still clearly visible on her body.

"Yeah, I love you," Lola replied, smiling and relieving all of Jake's fears. They showered together, Jake playfully sticking his cock back into Lola who just slapped it away giggling before getting dry and dressing in comfy house clothes.

"What should we do now baby girl?" Jake said. Lola just looked at him in confusion.

"I thought we were going to get our

puppies?" She replied, hoping that having dogs was still a plan. Having completely forgotten, Jake just laughed and held out his hand to Lola.

"Let's go now then, little one. We need to get you dressed," Jake said, excited to be getting dogs.

"But Daddy, I already am," Lola replied, but Jake already had her hand in his and was walking to the cupboard.

"Sit down," Jake instructed. He took out a pull up, her black stockings and black cotton dress, black sneakers and a red bandana for her hair.

"You are going to look so cute, baby girl," Jake said, powdering her pussy and pulling the pull-up on. He secured it in place by rolling the stockings up her hairless, soft legs, and pulled her dress on over the top.

"Cute little emo girl, I love it!" Jake said, putting on her shoes before fixing the bandana in place. Lola stood up and walked to the mirror; she had to admit, Jake could pull an outfit together really well.

"What are you going to wear, Daddy?" Lola said, watching as Jake pulled on black jeans, a white t-shirt, and his sneakers, a snapback cap, and a red bomber jacket.

"You forgot this, Daddy," Lola said, passing him his cologne. He smelt like money and responsibility, and Lola loved how he picked her up in one quick motion and carried her like a princess to the truck.

Chapter 8

Two months had passed since Lola and Jake had picked the dogs up from the shelter. Now they were the proud owners of two large Bullmastiffs. One white called Leo and a tan one called Nix. Although to everyone they came into contact with, they showed aggression; they loved Lola and Jake, who had spent all their free time training the two boys to be powerful protective dogs. Lola had also decided to resign from her job at the grocery store and had given an anonymous tip-off to the police as to when a possible drug deal would go down. While she had made just over $100,000 for her part in the deal, she hadn't taken the $30,000 that was collecting in the hole in the wall and knew that the money along with the drugs would be enough to convict Kane and get him off her back.

"What if he does put the pictures of you

around town?" Jake asked when he came home for lunch. Leo and Nix jumped up to follow him into the kitchen were Lola had made soup and pies for lunch, knowing that once they were finished, they would be given the rest.

"Honestly, at this point, I don't even care. I want to be rid of him. Whatever it takes," Lola said, serving Jake lunch. She had moved in with him now that the fence had been finished and the dogs could follow a series of violent commands at Jake or Lola's instruction. It did scare Lola to have such powerful dogs roaming freely around, but whenever she lay on the floor, they would come over to her and lay down on either side of her while she played or colored.

"It would certainly raise some eyebrows," Jake said, patting the dogs while he waited for his soup to cool.

"Daddy, let's just live our life," Lola said, coming to sit on his lap. She lifted up the back of her skirt, showing him her pantyless pussy and giggled as he quickly turned her around and bent her over the table.

"Such a dirty girl," Jake said, pulling his cock out of his work pants and slapping it against her ass cheek, making it stiff. He grabbed the large slice of pie in his hand, took a considerable mouthful before putting it back down and slapping Lola's ass with his hand.

"Bounce for Daddy," he ordered, taking the sweet iced tea she had made and drinking while he watched her twerk against his dick. Groaning at how hard she was making him, he grabbed her hips and pulled her down on his cock, making her squeal as he locked his legs around hers, holding her in place.

"Daddy is going to have his dick up you while I eat," Jake said, bucking his hips slightly, making her feel him inside of her while he enjoyed his lunch.

Finishing his lunch, Jake carried Lola to the couch, his cock still deep inside of her and let her drop down on the sofa.

"Open that hole for Daddy," Jake

commanded, waiting for Lola to spread her pussy lips open for him. Jake just laughed.

"No, the other one," he said, making Lola's eyes go wide. She bit her bottom lip as she pulled her ass cheeks back, exposing herself for Jake's viewing pleasure before he slapped her hole with the tip of his cock.

"I don't have long, don't fight me," Jake said, forcing her ass to accept his cock. Hearing her moans and squeals only made him want her more as he began his slow onslaught, making her take all of him and holding it in her so she could be stretched the way he wanted.

"Oh, that sucks, baby girl, Daddy has to go, but tonight, you'll take Daddy until I am piping my thick sticky cream in every one of your pretty holes," Jake said, as his alarm to go back to work sounded. Slapping her ass loving, he pulled out, his cock still hard, aching for release as he put it back in his pants and walked out the door.

"Baby, Daddy's home, where's that pretty

little," Jake said, stopping as he walked into the living room to see Lola with her arms tied behind her back and a gag in her mouth. Leo and Nix were chained and muzzled, being secured to the floor by a metal stake.

"So nice of you to join us. I was just telling Lola that something very funny happened today. Do you know what it was?" Kane said with a sinister smile.

"No, what?" Jake growled back, looking at Lola trying to see if she was hurt.

"When I went to drop a package off, a package that Lola was meant to be looking after, the police were already there. It was like; I don't know, they knew about the spot or something. But this is the amusing thing, the only people who knew about the spot were me, Lola, and I am now assuming you," Kane said, standing up from his seated position on the couch. He kissed Lola's cheek as he passed her and took out a gun from the back of his pants and casually waved it in Jake's face.

"So my question is this. Who is going to die today?" Kane said, pointing at Nix and firing.

"No!" Jake yelled, seeing his beloved dog fall with a sudden thud. Jake lunged at Kane copping an uppercut that made Jake stumble backward.

"Now now, don't do anything too rash. I was practicing. It was you, or Lola who ratted me out to the cops and only the rat has to die. I thought I was rather reasonable actually," Kane smirked. Jake looked behind Kane to see Lola crying and straining against her restraints to try and free herself.

"I wouldn't do that sweetheart, I have used my last bit of patience with you," Kane said, pistol wiping Lola and making her scream. Leo barked like crazy, making both Jake and Lola afraid he would be next.

"Look, let's settle this like men," Jake said, trying to stop himself from shaking with fear.

"What do you have in mind? See who can make the bitch cum first?" Kane laughed, slapping Lola's tits.

"No. A fight. If you win, you can kill me, if you lose, you leave town and never return," Jake said, trying to sound dominating. Kane just laughed again before sizing Jake up. As he sneered, he put his gun down and quickly punched Jake in the mouth, making his lip bleed and blood fly, splattering onto the wall.

"I thought you said you wanted to fight?" Kane laughed. Jake blocked his next punch and threw several of his own before Kane blocked him and kicked his knee caps making Jake stumble backward. He grabbed the stake for support, knocking it to the ground on his way down and releasing Leo from his trap. Quickly grabbing the muzzle and pulling it off Leo's head, Jake got up and blocked the next three kicks from Kane.

"Leo, kill," Jake yelled, watching as his dog barked aggressively at Kane before grabbing his arm and biting down hard, crushing his forearm. Kane let out a mighty yell, trying to get to his gun with the dog tearing the flesh from his arm.

"Lola, baby, close your eyes," Jake said, as

he reached the gun first, pulled the trigger and waited for the ringing in his ears to stop.

"Leo, drop," Jake said, watching as the bloody mess that Kane had been reduced to lay motionless on the floor.

"Lola, baby girl, I'm going to untie you now, you have to promise not to scream when you open your eyes," Jake gently said as he untied Lola's wrists and took out the gag.

"Jake," she said, breathlessly pushing him out of the way and standing up.

"What have you done?" She quickly added, seeing Kane's dead body sprawled out on the floor. Jake turned to see that Kane was no longer a threat, and saw the Leo had gone to lay next to Nix.

"I know boy, come on," Jake said, looking Leo in the eye and waiting for him to make his way to Jake's side slowly. Jake took Lola's hand, and the three of them walked into the bedroom and closed the door.

"What are we supposed to do now?" Lola asked Jake who had to sit on his hands to stop them shaking.

"I don't know. I have a friend in the force, he owes me a favor," Jake said, not sure if what he was owed amounted to hiding a body. Lola just sighed a sigh of relief but knowing that what was to come next was even more dangerous.

"Someone will step up, and whoever does, will use our deaths as a way to prove their strength. Who is your friend?" Lola asked, hoping that it wasn't who she thought it was.

"Clive," Jake said, knowing that Lola and he had a history. Clive used to live next door to Lola and once Lola had seen him watching her get changed after gym class and from then on had referred to him as, *The Creep.*

"Oh, no, really?!" Lola exclaimed, annoyed that she had just gotten rid of one problem only to have another one emerge.

"He's the best chance that we have. Lola, we have the body of the biggest drug lord in Hollywood dead on our living room floor, I don't think we have too many options, do you?" Jake said, patting Leo's head. Lola just rolled her eyes and shook her head.

"Ok, you're right. Call *The Creep*," she said before standing and going to have a shower.

Chapter 9

"Jakey boy, how are you?" Clive asked, three hours later as he stepped out of his police car. Lola stood there, on the front steps watching Clive with narrowed eyes.

"Lola," Clive said, nodding to her but walking straight past her and into the living room.

"So, as I said, some stuff got real, and well, this happened," Jake said, gesturing to the dead Kane in the semi-dried pool of blood on the wooden floors of the living room.

"Dude, do you know who this is?!" Clive excitedly said, his mouth gaping open.

"No, I just came home with Lola to find him and my dog like this," Jake said, following the story that he and Lola had developed.

"So weird. I'm going to have to take a couple of photos. Yeah, I can see here that there was a break in, which makes sense considering that you weren't home at the time," Clive said, walking around the space and winking at Lola who had come to stand next to Jake.

"Oh, the old prom king and queen finally back together. I tell you what; Jake was a mess when you left, Lola," Clive teased making Jake laugh.

"What can I say, it's love," Jake said, holding onto Lola tight as they watched Clive take some more photos.

"I'll get the boys here to get rid of this and to clean it up for you. It must be so weird coming home to see this," Clive said, looking suspiciously at the two of them.

"Weird. Kinda like when you," Lola said, before Clive cut her off, not wanting to go down memory lane.

"Well, as long as you two are fine, that's the main thing. I'll need to take your statements, but then you'll be free to go," Clive said, as they followed him to the front door.

"Of course, thanks again for coming to soon, I didn't know what to do," Jake said, holding out his hand to shake Clive's.

"Oh, Jakey boy, anything for you," Clive said, smiling the same sinister smile Kane had only hours before.

"Do you think he knows that was all bullshit?" Lola said the moment they were out of the police station and back in the truck.

"I don't think so. Clive is a creep, yes, but he is more impressed that he was the one to find the body. This'll be good for his career, and that's all he cares about," Jake replied, hoping that this marked the end of the ordeal. Lola just looked out the window and watched as the trees fly by, wishing that she didn't feel the need to cry. It had been a hard day. They kind she had never thought would be one of hers.

"Do you need Daddy, little girl," Jake said, sensing she was close to tears. Lola just nodded and reached for his hand, nuzzling into his shoulder and letting her tears fall.

"I'm sorry Daddy, it's all my fault," Lola mumbled, wiping her eyes on Jake's blue flannel shirt. He kissed her head and looked at her in the eye, coming to a stop on the side of the road.

"No, it's not your fault. You did a dumb thing at the start of all this, yes, but you didn't make him do all those things. You didn't make him hurt you, that's on him. He got what he deserved," Jake said, watching as the first of the winter snow fell onto the windscreen.

"Let's go home; we can watch the snow from our bed, and you can cuddle with Daddy all night little girl," Jake said, to a clapping Lola.

"Here's your hot chocy, baby girl," Jake said, bringing the warm liquid into the bedroom. He had put it in Lola's favorite sippy cup and watched as her eyes lit up instantly.

"Thank you, Daddy," Lola replied obediently before reaching out her arms to take the cup in her hands.

"I love this. My happy baby girl, the snow, Leo by the fire. Tomorrow I want to take you shopping for some new clothes; you'll be Daddy's little snow bunny this winter, baby girl," Jake said, imagining how she would look. Lola could see he was enjoying his fantasy as he grew harder under the blankets.

"Daddy," Lola giggled, pushing his cock down and making him laugh.

"What can I say, baby girl, Daddy likes what he sees," Jake replied, taking Lola's cup away from her and placing it down on the floor.

"How about you show Daddy why I should buy you everything you want tomorrow," Jake said, reaching out to touch her. He ran his hands over the top of her pink long-sleeved sweater, enjoying how the fluffy material felt as he cupped her tits.

"I like this no bra rule I gave you, it's good," Jake said, groping at her predatorily. Lola just giggled as she tried to pull away.

"No, you'll give Daddy everything little

one," Jake said, taking both her wrists in one of his hands as the other hand reached under her sweater to touch her naked skin.

"So soft and warm," he muttered, getting lost as his hand was filled with Lola's left then right breast. Lifting the sweater off her, he sat back and placed her on top of him, watching as she began moving in a slow rhythm on his lap.

"I could just slide into you right now," Jake said, getting lost in Lola's eyes as he slowly pulled his cock and swollen balls from his black sweat pants. Lifting the front of Lola's short skirt up, he watched as his cock gently smacked the front of her shaven pussy, pink puffy pussy lips parting around his thick shaft.

"Don't stop," Jake said, loving how Lola bent forward to rest her hands on his chest. She lifted up slightly, enough for Jake to position his cock under her and lifted his hips up, taking his prize. Lola's pussy, as wet as ever, never denying him as she took him in one slow go, letting him fill her to her hilt and tightening her cunt around him.

"Hold on, baby girl," Jake said as he picked Lola up and carried her to the wall, pressing against her as he began to fuck her in the air. Holding her up by her ass, Lola wrapped her arms around Jake's neck and held on as he had his way with her. Her body becoming limp in his arms as he used her, pounding hard while his balls were wet with the cum that dripped from her cunt, and into her ass.

"God you are perfect," Jake said, cumming again. He lay her on her tummy, pulling up a pair of lace panties taking her by surprise.

"Don't you dare fucking move," Jake said, straddling her thighs as he came to sit behind her. He ran his hands over her now panty covered ass, feeling the smooth, cool material and watching as his cock dripped cum onto them. He lifted the left side of the panties, fingering Lola's closed cunt and wriggling his finger inside of her, enjoying how tight she was. Taking his finger out, he pulled on the panties until they were up her ass crack before sliding his cock along the crevice he had made, pushing his big mushroom tip along her wet crack, the panties holding his rod in place.

"I just want to fuck you," Jake moaned as he began humping her from behind, pushing his cock into whichever hole would have him first. Her cunt opened around his shaft, and he plowed inside, keeping Lola's thighs squeezed together and panties on. Getting onto his knees, Jake fucked her deeper, pushing her head down and pulling out just as he came, deciding to cum on her panties instead.

"Yeah, such a dirty slut for Daddy aren't you," Jake said before going back for more. This time, he shoved his dick into her ass, making her scream as he forced her open.

"Take it, bitch, you love it, you love being used like a dirty whore; don't you," Jake said, taking Lola's hands and filling them with his balls.

"Play with my sack," he instructed as he pushed into her, pushing his balls into her hands and holding himself inside of her as he came. Pulling out, he turned her over and looked at her before standing on top of her and lowering his balls into her mouth.

"Open wide for Daddy," Jake said, placing his hand on Lola's throat and choking her gently as she sucked his balls until he came again, this time letting his cum cover her tits and tummy.

"Good girl," Jake said, standing back up and walking over to the bed and fishing for something in the sheets. He took out a chastity belt which had a vibrating dildo and butt plug, before also taking out a diaper from the cupboard.

"Come to Daddy, princess, I have a special treat for you," Jake said, grabbing Lola's ankle and pulling her to him. He didn't bother lubing it as it slid into her holes easily, making him laugh. Next, he locked it in place, telling her that it would stay on all night. Taking the diaper, he added extra padding, forcing her thighs to spread wide and dressed her in her white bunny onesie. Lola could feel her cunt ache for release as Jake only turned it on a low setting, making her grind on his thigh, desperate to cum.

"No, no cummies for you tonight little girl, Daddy is too tired," Jake said, pulling the sheets down and tucking her into bed. He held her through the night, stroking her nipples and making her suck him off multiple times, before making her fall asleep with his cock in her mouth.

Chapter 10

"And in breaking news, the body of drug kingpin, Kane Jones, has been found in a turn of interesting events as the body was found during a drug raid in a small town just outside of Hollywood," the reporter said as Lola and Jake watched the nightly news. Turning the tv off, Jake looked at Lola who just burst out laughing.

"Oh my god," Lola squealed with excitement that they had gotten away with Kane's murder.

"Holy shit. Well, that's that then," Jake said, turning to face Lola.

"What are we meant to do now?" Lola said, for the first time not having anything to either run from or set in place, and she was bored instantly.

"What should we do now?" Lola said again, excitement in her eyes. Jake just double took as his head spun with what on earth Lola could mean.

"Um, relax?" Jake suggested as though Lola had lost her mind.

"No, come on, let's go out, celebrate, get wasted and fuck in your truck," Lola said, grabbing Jake's hands and bouncing on the couch.

"Baby, no, I've got work in the morning. Maybe we should think about you going back to work now that Kane is out of the picture," Jake said, deflating Lola's enthusiasm instantly.

"Yeah, my thoughts exactly," Lola said before getting up and walking to the bathroom.

"We can do something fun on the weekend, baby," Jake said, receiving a fake smile from Lola.

"Yeah, I'd like that," Lola said as she shut the door slowly before locking it. She looked in the mirror and wondered how much longer she could live a life like this with Jake. Sure, he was kind, supportive, loyal, and loving. But he was boring. There was nothing remotely exciting about how he wanted to live, and if it weren't for the way he fucked her, Lola would have left him long ago. Turning the water on, Lola slid down the wall and sat on the floor, letting the hot water hit her body and warm her skin. She thought about what she wanted to do next. *Why do you always have to be looking for your next hit of adrenaline?* Lola asked herself, annoyed that she couldn't feel happy with a simple life. She was only coming back to this town to try and run on her own, if she hadn't reunited with Jake, she would have been happily rolling in cash and living for the moment like she loved to do. *That's it, I live for the moment, and Jake lives for, a longer moment I guess,* Lola thought as she began soaping her body, feeling lonely and bored all at the same time.

Lola decided to spend the next few days looking for work, convincing herself that if she could find a job somewhere somewhat exciting, it would curb her need to be searching for her next hit continually. Walking from store to store, Lola realized that nothing excited her. As she walked up and down the main street in town, she sighed, sitting on a bench and looking out onto the road.

"You look like you could use this," a voice said coming behind her and sitting next to her. Lola groaned and rolled her eyes.

"And here I was thinking this day couldn't get any worse," Lola said, looking down at the cup Clive was offering her.

"I could always arrest you, spice it up a little when I slot you," he said, taking Lola's hand and making her hold the cup.

"Drink," he said, lifting her compliant hands, bringing the cup to her lips.

"You're such a seedy fuck," Lola said, eyeing Clive as she beginning sipping the coffee but pulling the cup away from her almost immediately.

"There's Irish Crème in this?!" Lola accused looking at Clive as though he had lost his mind. He just laughed and drunk his, before throwing the empty cup in the trash, leaning across with his big stomach pressing onto Lola's tits and looking her in the eye.

"Yeah," he said, smirking when Lola rolled her eyes and took another sip.

"You looked like you could use it. I've been watching you," Clive said, getting cut off by Lola.

"I bet you have," she said plainly, sipping again.

"I've been watching you walk up and down here, what are you trying to do? Get a job?" Clive asked, ignoring her cheep insult. Looking at him out of the corner of her eye, Lola sighed, dropping her guard and sighing again before turning to look at him.

"Yeah, Jake thought it would be a good idea to go back to work," Lola said, resting her head on her hand, her elbow resting on the back of the bench. Clive just nodded.

"And no luck yet?" he asked, readjusting his holster.

"Nope," Lola replied, reaching back and throwing her empty cup in the trash.

"Well, we need someone to file things back at the station?" Clive suggested making Lola laugh.

"And you have the power just to hire someone with zero experience?" Lola questioned, raising her eyebrow. Clive smirked.

"It's a really easy job, doesn't really take a lot of training. Plus, we aren't a unit, have you ever seen more than me and the three other guys in uniform?" Clive said, making Lola think. *No, actually, I haven't,* she thought, a smile spreading across her lips.

"When can I start?" She asked, Clive, looking her up and down, eyeing her breasts.

"What are you doing now?" He asked, standing up and cracking his back.

"Um, actually, I'm a little tipsy right now," Lola replied, laughing despite herself.

"Then you'll fit right in," Clive replied, walking towards the old police house at the end of the main street followed by Lola.

"Hey, Jake, I found a job!" Lola yelled as she ran into the house. Running into the bedroom, she saw Jake sitting up and working on his computer.

"Did you hear? I have a new job," Lola repeated, watching as Jake patted the spot beside him.

"Nice work, baby girl. Where?" Jake asked, putting his laptop down and closing the lid.

"Cop shop, I am going to do the filing and some paperwork," Lola said, proud of herself for finding a job she didn't completely hate.

"Wow, really? Don't you need experience or like, qualifications for something like that?" Jake questioned Lola who just shook her head no, her hair swaying as she excitedly bounced on the bed.

"You wanna fuck now, Daddy?" Lola teased, turning around and showing him her red lace thong as she pulled up her black leather skirt.

"Not right now sweetie, Daddy has to finish this first. Go into the nursery and take out what you want to wear tonight, I think you've been a big girl for long enough today," Jake said, making Lola pout and whine.

"Daddy," Lola said, drawing out the word, coping a slap across her face.

"Don't make Daddy mad; I've told you what to do, go do it," Jake growled, before gently pushing Lola from the bed and bringing his laptop back onto his lap and continuing to work. Lola rolled her eyes and walked from the room as her phone vibrated in her pocket. Taking it out and looking at the series of photos that Clive had sent her, she bit her bottom lip. *He is just a dickhead. He doesn't know anything*; she told herself as she wondered if Clive had somehow figured out her kink. She looked at the adult baby outfits he had sent her, along with the message, *I think you'd look adorable in all of these.* Putting her phone away, she walked into the nursery and searched for her teddy bear onesie, enjoying how the woman looked wearing the same one in the photo Clive had just sent her.

"Oh, no, I was thinking something more like this," Jake said, suddenly appearing behind her making her jump. He put the onesie away and took out a pink sailor outfit, placing it over the side of her crib and pulling her to the floor and beginning to undress her.

"Daddy, I don't want that one," Lola said,

pushing his hands away. Jake just calmly walked to the cupboard and took out the silk ties and whip, striking her thighs as he returned, making Lola roll around trying to escape him.

"That's why I thought I'd need these," Jake said, tieing her wrists to her ankles, exposing her pussy to him.

"This might remind you not to complain to me," Jake said, whipping her pussy gently, but making her squeal all the same.

"Shh shh, baby girl, I'm not going to hurt you, it's just a little reminder," Jake said, smiling as Lola stopped moving and bit her lip as he brought the whip down on her sensitive skin once more. Tossing the whip to the side, he untied her and carried her to the bathroom, running the shower water over her body and soaping her generously.

"Daddy, you're tickling me," Lola giggled, making Jake rub her more vigorously. He rinsed her off, dried her down, and carried her back into the nursery.

"Lay down for Daddy," Jake instructed,

pointing to the fluffy pink rug in the middle of the room. Lola crawled to the middle of the circle rug and laid on her back as she watched Jake walk around the room. He collected her diaper, powder and sailor outfit, as well as her white thigh high socks.

"You know what to do, don't you baby girl," Jake said, pressing he pacifier to her lips and making her mouth open. Sucking loudly, Lola lifted her bottom as Jake placed her thick diaper under her and powdered her generously. Tickling her nipples by flicking them until she giggled, Jake then fastened the tabs of the diaper and rolled her socks up her thighs, pulling them slightly higher than they needed to go. He lifted her onto his lap and held her on top of his knees as he clipped the outfit up Lola's back and ruffled the skirt over her diaper.

"Daddy," Lola said, blushing as Jake toyed with her. He smiled as he placed her back down on the floor and walked over to the rocking chair, sitting down and watching as she started to color in her coloring in books.

"Daddy has to go out of town for a couple of nights baby," he said, rocking back and forth and waiting for Lola to turn around and look at him.

"Why, Daddy?" Lola asked, taking her pacifier out and putting it down on her coloring in table.

"There's an excellent conference happening next week that I think would be beneficial for the business," Jake said, patting his lap and watching as Lola crawled to him. Bending down, he picked her up and placed her on his lap, rocking her in his arms.

"Ok, Daddy," Lola said, burying her face in his neck.

"It's ok baby; you'll be fine. You have your new job, and Leo, you won't even know I'm gone," Jake said to which Lola doubted very much.

Chapter 11

Jake was going to be away for five days. He had told her he would message, but as the second day of his trip started, she hadn't received one text despite messaging him several times. Bored, Lola knew why she had agreed to meet up with Clive after dark and outside of work, but she wasn't sure why it excited her so much. He wasn't like Jake or even Kane. Sure he was handsome but in an ugly sexy kind of way. His thick black beard made him look intimidating, and his hairy, big body made him look like a cave-man. She hated herself for wondering how big his dick was, but she was sure he wouldn't shave there if he didn't shave anywhere else.

Maybe he has figured out that it was Jake who had killed Kane, Lola nervously thought as she approached the quiet bar. Opening the door her heels were the only sound to be heard as she made her way to the back booth Clive was already sitting in.

"Hi," Lola said to Clive, who just pushed a phone across the table to her. Lola recognized it immediately.

"You won't believe the kind of filth that was on his phone. You do know who I'm talking about, don't you?" Clive said, finishing his second beer and ordering another.

"It's not what it looks like," Lola said making Clive augh.

"Oh, it's exactly what it looks like. Why do you think I sent you those outfit suggestions?" He replied, sitting back and admiring the dress Lola had worn. It was red, short but not sluty and he wondered how easy it would be to get her naked.

"Look. Jake is a good guy; he would be ruined if these photos were to emerge," Clive said, looking at Lola predatorily.

"What do you want?" Lola said, knowing what Clive was going to say before he opened his mouth. In all the years she had lived next to Clive, the only thing he had ever wanted was to get close to her. Now, sitting here in the empty, dark bar with the perfect blackmail, Lola knew she was about to give him what he had always wanted. Clive stroked his thick black beard and placed his hand out of sight. Lola knew it would be on his cock, stroking it over his trousers by the way his bicep was moving.

"I want you to get on your knees right now and suck my dick," Clive said without skipping a beat. Lola looked around. Clive must have paid off the barkeeper because not even he was insight anymore. Sighing, Lola moved over to where Clive was sitting, stopping when he reached out to grab her hand.

"No, I want you to sit here, and let me touch your tits," he said, changing his mind. Clive reached out his hand and groaned as he cupped Lola's pushed out tits. She knew she had to give him a good time, or those photos would be everywhere. Staying still and quiet, Clive groped at her while he drank, watching the football on the tv as his cock grew hard.

"I don't even know where I want to start with you," he whispered in her ear, reaching under her dress and feeling her thighs and cunt.

"Spread your thighs for, Daddy," Clive said, smirking as he said, Daddy.

"That's what you like isn't it, a big strong Daddy to look after you, little Lola," Clive said, feeling how Lola's breathing quicken. She hated herself for enjoying this, but as his big hands pawed at her, she could feel her cunt begin to moisten.

"Well, tonight you'll have a real Daddy. Yeah, I want to get you all sloppy with my cum, have your fingers running through my fur as I breed you," Clive said, unzipping his trousers and grabbing the back of Lola's head, making her stare at his long pubes covering his balls which pushed out around the un-cut cock he jerked in his hand.

"You are going to want me again and again. You are going to wish you had given yourself to me sooner after I'm done with you," Clive said, pushing Lola's head down and rubbing his foreskin over her lips.

"The longer you fight me, the longer I'm going to keep you," Clive said, holding Lola's nose closed and making her open her mouth for air. He took the opportunity to stick his fat cock into her mouth, pulling out his balls and rubbing them as she was forced to suck him. Clive only had to pull Lola's head up and down a few times before she opened her throat and took him until his balls were touching her lips, his pubes tickling her face.

"Holy shit, baby, yeah, suck your Daddy," Clive said, surprised Lola was taking him without his force.

"Oh yeah, you like Daddy, don't you. You want to suck the cum out of this dick," Clive said, reaching down to grope Lola's tits once again. Suddenly pulling her head back, Clive pulled his cock from her mouth as he came. Holding her jaw open, he shot his thick creamy load down her, making her eyes water as it tickled the back of her throat. Clive held her in position until he was finished, his cock limp but his adrenaline pumping.

"Come with me," Clive said, taking Lola's hand and leading her out of the bar. As he grabbed his coat by the door, he put his cock away and zipped up his trousers before pushing the door open and leading Lola to his car.

"I know you liked that, I could feel it, you want me," Clive said as he drove through the night. He lifted Lola's dress and caressed her soft thigh while he spoke.

"Look at you; you can't even deny it," Clive happily said as he saw Lola spread her thighs for him. Reaching for her sweet spot, Clive pulled her thong aside and dipped his two fingers into her wet gash.

"I told you, I knew you were wet for me," Clive said, laughing as Lola rolled her eyes at him.

"They only reason I am letting you have your fun is that I want those photos deleted," Lola tried to say although her words came out in moans as she let Clive fiddle with her clit and pussy lips.

Driving over a bump, Clive used the opportunity to slide his finger into her cunt and force her to sit on his hand while his fingers wriggled inside of her for the rest of the drive.

"Where are we going?" Lola said breathlessly as her orgasm built inside of her.

"Just a little further," Clive said as he drove into the woods. Lola didn't see where she was as she closed her eyes and came in Clive's hand, making him laugh in satisfaction.

"Follow me," Clive said as he took his hand away, turned the car off, and opened the door. Lola followed, running around to grab his hand, surprising both Clive and herself.

"What, I'm scared," Lola said in a bratty tone she hadn't realized she had. Clive just grunted as the feeling of dominance flowed through him as he led her deeper into the woods, wrapping his hairy arm around her and pulling her into his chubby stomach as they walked.

Stopping at a clearing, a modest wood cabin with smoke coming from the chimney made Lola stop in her tracks.

"I know this place," she said, trying to remember when she had been here.

"I know you do. It's where we use to play," Clive said, happy she remembered.

"You've done it up?" Lola asked, following Clive inside. She looked around the living space; the rustic feel of the cabin made her feel right at home. The animal hides on the roughly leveled wooden floor, the big soft sofa in front of the fire and the upstairs loft made Lola annoyed she liked it so much.

"You're not going to need this anymore," Clive said, coming behind her and taking her coat from her shoulders. He wrapped his arm around her waist and flung her over his shoulder as he carried her caveman style to the rugs in front of the fire.

"Take your shoes off," he instructed, sitting on the sofa and watching as she obeyed him. Lola rested both her hands on his knees as she kicked off her heels, showing him down her dress. Clive leaned back, his large body melting into the material of the sofa, making him look soft and even chubbier.

"Now your dress," he said, reaching up to turn Lola around, so she was facing away from him. He watched as her dress slipped off her hips, the fire illuminating her slender form. Clive smiled as he saw she wasn't wearing a bra and snorted with excitement.

"You are just a fat, hairy pig," Lola said, as Clive grabbed her arm and made her sit on his lap.

"And how does it feel to know you want me more than your pretty boy?" Clive replied, pulling her back onto him and holding her there, her arms pinned by her sides, her ass being poked with his big, soft cock. Lola just squirmed on his lap, making him laugh.

"Do you like pretending you don't want it? Does that turn you on?" Clive said, making Lola annoyed that he could read her so well.

"Is that why you stayed with Kane for all those years? So you were able to be taken by him whenever he wanted his dick wet? Do you really think I don't know that you two had been fucking for years before you came back here? I see you for who you really are Lola. A dirty, horny, desperate little girl who just wants to be taken by the biggest, baddest Daddy she can find," Clive said, letting Lola go as he quickly reached down and stabbed his cock into her making her scream.

"Bounce on it, show me that I'm right," Clive said, as Lola began riding his cock, bending forward to grab his knees and grind down on him with desperate ambition as she fucked his cock. She knew he was right; she had known it the minute she had enjoyed him watching her. Calling him a creep had only ever turned her on. She wondered how he could have seen it when no-one else seemed to. Jake had missed it, Kane had been too dumb to realize, and yet it was the fat, hairy cop who had forced his cock inside her which she now was willingly taking who had picked it from the start.

"Daddy's sweet little girl," Clive said, taking

her in his hands and bouncing her on top of him with a strength that surprised Lola. Letting her legs go limp as Clive lifted and dropped her body on his lap, Lola felt her cunt gush, covering Clive's pants as she squirted for the first time.

"Clive, I," Lola gasped, unsure of how he would respond but happily stopping her fears as he exploded inside of her, mixing his cum with hers.

"Oh yeah, that's it," Clive said, as Lola's body dripped with sweat from the heat of the room and the fuck she was taking. Waiting until she had stopped quivering, Clive gently lifted her off him, feeling his trousers get covered in cum as Lola's cunt gushed again with the removal of his monster rod.

"I've never done that before," Lola said, fixing her thong back in place and feeling little for the first time with him. Clive looked at her, impressed with himself.

"Well, you have now," he said, standing up and stretching, his shirt lifting to reveal his furry stomach.

"You want to go? I'll get the phone, you can delete the photos," Clive said, reaching into his pocket and passing Lola the phone. She held it in her hands and watched as Clive went to the fridge and took out a beer. Looking down at the photos of her and Jake, Lola smiled as she deleted the images before passing the phone back to Clive.

"I don't want to go," Lola said, wrapping her arms around the big Daddy in front of her and sighing in contented bliss.

"I told you, you wouldn't want to leave," Clive laughed as he stroked her hair before placing a finger in her mouth.

"But here's the thing, if you stay, my cock is going to fuck you over and over. You're my prize, my trophy, and I am going to use you all night," Clive said, chugging his beer before putting the empty bottle on the bench and grabbing Lola's small wrist in his big hand. He led her back to the sofa, this time pushing her onto the floor and standing over the top of her, pushing her head back until she couldn't move away from him anymore.

"Where do you think you are going?" Clive laughed, taking his balls and rubbing them over Lola's face until her mouth opened and she began sucking them.

"That's it, suck on Daddy's big balls, you'll learn to do that every night now that I've got you," Clive said letting his dick flop over Lola's face as she gagged on his sack. He watched as the fire roared and Lola obediently went from sucking his cock to his sack and back to his cock as he repeatedly pushed himself into her mouth.

"Get on all fours," he instructed, watching as Lola turned on the spot for him. He lay down on the floor and began sucking her nipples before taking her hips in his hands and lifting her up, laughing as her arms gave way and she fell on top of his hairy chest as he lowered her pelvis down onto his. He held her, waiting until she relaxed enough to almost fall asleep before parting her thighs and sliding his thick snake up her cunt, taking her by surprise.

"You didn't think I was done with you, did you?" Clive said as he began to fuck her. Rolling over, he liked how his body pressed into hers, engulfing her as he pumped in and out of her, her hole taking him more easily, her moans only encouraging him. He panted as he fucked her, pushing her down with his stomach as his balls slapped against her asshole with each thrust he used to fill her. Cumming suddenly, he squirted into her, pulling his limp cock out, again satisfied.

"Oh, you are good Lola. I can see why Jake likes you," Clive said, sitting on the floor and lifting Lola up under her armpits and pulling her body onto his lap. Cradling her in his arms, they watched as the fire burned, ambers flicking and crackling before he lay her down on her tummy. He placed one of his legs over her back as the other one made way for Lola's head.

"You know what to do," Clive said, flopping his meat in her face as she opened her mouth and began sucking him off once more as he reached down and slapped her ass lazily making it jiggle over and over.

Chapter 12

"What am I suppose to do now?" Lola said the moment Clive woke up the next morning. He yawned before answering her and smiled as he felt his wood harden. He had dressed her in a short baby doll dress that was one size too small for her breasts, making them pull the material tightly over her chest. He liked to make his women look like sluts, and as he wobbled his cock with one hand and reached for her pussy with the only, he liked that Lola was the biggest slut of them all. She wriggled her pussy down onto his fingers, feeling him securing her cunt to his palm and rubbing her with his opened hand as his fingers moved inside of her.

"You can start by taking care of this," he said, pulling the sheets off of the both of them and pushing her head down onto his shaft. Rolling her eyes, Lola opened her mouth and began sucking the pre-cum from his cock.

"I guess you have two options, you either break up with Jake, or you go back to him, knowing that he will never be able to give you what I can," Clive said, taking his cock from her throat and pushing it down the side of her mouth, enjoying how the skin of her cheek pushed out against him.

"Either way, the choice is yours," Clive said, shooting down the side of her mouth, making her feel like she was being drenched. Clive pulled his cock from her lips, taking his time to rub the tip over her lips, watching how they pouted around his tip, coating her lips in his cream.

"Up you come," he said, finally taking his cock from her face. He pulled his fingers from her, pushing them into her mouth and making her suck her juices off before groping her tits over her dress. Forcing himself into her tight cunt, Clive laughed as she tried to refuse him, only making him spear her harder, flicking her clit with his fingertip, making her pussy wetter than she wanted it to be.

"There you go," he groaned as her muscles gave away, allowing him access into her throbbing cunt. He held her there, on top of him before he slowly rocked back and forth, humping her like she was an animal on heat, and he was the beast who wanted her.

"Daddy," Lola said as she was fucked, making Clive take her arms and pin them behind her back as he mounted her from behind.

"Oh yeah, baby girl, who's your Daddy," Clive said as he smashed her raw, feeling her cunt go dry as she was over fucked. He pulled out of her and cradled her in his arms, his hairy chest and stomach sweaty as he held her close.

"Do you want to see just how cute Daddy can make you?" Clive said, piquing Lola's curiosity. She slowly nodded her head as Clive let her go, getting up to go into his cupboard. Taking out a teddy bear diaper, fluffy brown teddy bear onesie, and a white pacifier, Clive smiled at Lola as he came back to the bed.

"I've got to get you all cleaned up before I make you my precious little one," Clive said, taking Lola's hand and leading her into the bathroom.

"I'm surprised how much space is here," Lola said, taking in the large bathroom. The bathtub was big enough for three people, and the shower was modern, the type without doors. The wall length window overlooked the woods, and Lola smiled as Clive lifted her into the bath.

"I had no idea you were so strong," Lola said, as Clive sat on the edge of the bath with his legs in the water. He smiled as he watched her play with the bubbles.

"What kind of things do you like when you are my little girl?" Clive asked, making Lola swim over to him and rest her head on his thigh. She thought before shrugging her shoulders.

"No one has ever asked me that before, I don't really know. I guess I like coloring in, Daddy cuddles and movies. I like drinking from a sippy cup, and I have a couple of toys," Lola replied.

"Well, we will have to get you a whole lot more, I can't have my little angel only having one or two stuffies," Clive said, seeing his cock go hard.

"Daddy, I know what to do," Lola said, opening her mouth and sucking him deeply down her throat.

"Oh, good girl," Clive said, holding her head to him, moving his pelvis forward until he heard her gag and splashing water on the floor.

"Tell Jake that you have to break up with him. That you've found a real man who can give you what he can't," Clive said, pulling his cock from Lola's mouth and replacing it with his balls.

"Tell him; you need a real Daddy. Not some guy who can't see what you really need," he groaned, his cum splashing in the water. Lola pulled back from him and watched as Clive got into the water with her. He lay down in the tub, making her turn away from him as he positioned her on top. Pushing his cock into her without her complaining for the first time since last night, he trusted his pelvis up, making Lola bounce hard on the meat that filled her. Water splashed out of the tub as Lola was taken, being forced to ride the hairy, chubby bear of a man only making her cunt ache as he overpowered her again.

"I hate that I love this," Lola said, dipping her head and allowing Clive to play with her asshole. Clive just smirked, as he teased her rim, before turning her over to lay on top of him.

"Well, you can pretend you hate it all you want, we both know you really do love it," he said, placing his big paw of a hand on her ass cheek and groping it as she rested her head on his chest.

"Hey, how was your trip?" She asked, making Jake look up from his computer as she walked into the office. Her head was a mess. She looked at the man in front of her, with his kind eyes and gentle smile and hated herself for the knowledge she carried in her heart.

"Yeah, awesome, just what I needed actually. How was your time?" Jake asked, trying to subtly turning off his computer screen.

"It was fine, I'm glad to be back here though," she lied, Clive had to practically kick her out of the house to get her to leave.

"Well, that's good. I missed you," Jake said also lying, standing up and walking out from behind his desk to hug her. Feeling his body against hers, a shiver ran down Lola's spine.

"Are you cold sweetie? Do you want to turn the fire on?" Jake said, making Lola annoyed he couldn't just figure out what she wanted. Smiling, Lola just shook her head, kissing him on the cheek.

"I think I'll just have a shower; I'm tired. I went for a run this morning, and you know that wrecks me for the day," she said, turning and walking out of the room.

He killed a man for you. He was your high school sweetheart. You weren't even coming back for him, Lola said to herself as the warm water ran down her exhausted body. Clive had made sure she had no bruising on her body, but she could still feel him on her. The way his hands choked her throat, his cock squirting inside of her, the way he pawed at her making her feel small and helpless. Her pussy couldn't get enough of him. The thought of Jake entered her mind, and she didn't know how she would tell him that it was over.

"Knock knock," Jake said from the doorway of the bathroom ripping Lola from her thoughts. Turning around, she saw him standing there with her towel.

"You've been in here for an hour, I think you should get out," Jake said, opening the shower door and passing her the towel.

"Really? It's felt like five minutes," Lola laughed.

"Are you sure you are ok? You seem distant," Jake asked, sitting down on the floor of the bathroom while he watched her dry off. Lola just shook her head, making her wet hair flick him with water.

"Maybe you need some Daddy time," Jake said as he got up and took the towel from Lola's hands.

"Or maybe I needed a text or a phone call

while you were away!" Lola suddenly exclaimed, pushing Jake away. He just stood there and nodded.

"Yeah, sorry about that, the time just went so fast that I almost couldn't keep up myself," Jake said, making Lola roll her eyes.

"Whatever, I don't even care," Lola said, feeling Jake grab her upper arm.

"Yeah you do, say it, say you missed Daddy," Jake said, waiting for Lola to obey him.

"But I didn't," Lola said, refusing to give him what he wanted.

"You didn't miss me?" Jake said, pretending to be surprised. He knew Lola missed him, and as he felt between her thighs, he smirked with how wet she was.

"Show Daddy," Jake said, pulling Lola's thighs apart, surprised when she refused him.

"No, I don't want to right now," Lola said, not wanting the memory of Clive's cock to be replaced by Jake's just yet. Jake just let her go and walked out of the room, making Lola wonder if he was mad.

"Then you'll be teased until you are begging to be fucked," Jake said coming back into the room and lubing up her double penetrating chastity belt.

"Daddy," Lola said, pushing his hands away.

"It's pointless to refuse me. If you don't let Daddy stuff you with his cock, you can take this instead," Jake said, pulling the belt up Lola's thighs and spreading her pussy lips and ass cheeks as the toys filled her, making her gasp. Locking it in place, Jake took some heating lube and rubbed in over Lola's clit, enjoying how the belt forced her lips to spread around the material. He picked her up, hearing her moan as he put the setting on a medium vibration and placed her down on the floor, making her face him as he sat on the couch.

"Open wide for Daddy, I told you I would fill your holes," Jake said cuffing Lola's wrists behind her back and pushing his veiny cock into her mouth. Pumping her like she was on loan, he came quickly, not bothering to pull out and feeling Lola's throat convulse around his meat.

"Yeah, Daddy's dirty girl, you like to be fucked. Don't you," Jake said, reaching for Lola's tits and fiddling with her as he pulled his cock from her lips.

"Swallow," Jake said, seeing the mouthful of cum Lola had in her mouth. He put his balls in her mouth, holding her throat, feeling her swallow his cum and gagging on his sack as they were sucked into her throat.

"Oh yeah, give it to Daddy," Jake said, slapping her ass and watching as she wiggled it for him, her own pussy juices beginning to drip from her open cunt.

"I should record this shit, you are such a dirty little slut, yeah, make it clap baby," Jake said as Lola's ass began to jiggle as the orgasm, Jake was forcing on her dripped from her.

"You are such a flirt, teasing me until I pound you," Jake said, sticking his cock back in her mouth making her suck him until he came again. This time, he unlocked her belt, pulled it from her aggressively as he shoved his cumming cock inside of her, and held her down as he emptied his balls deep inside of her.

"Good girl," Jake said, patting Lola's head dismissingly as he got up and walked into the bathroom and shut the door, leaving Lola on the floor by herself.

He has never done that before, Lola though, bringing her knees to her chest and reaching for her phone.

Daddy, Lola text to Clive, wanting not to feel so alone. Happy when he replied straight away.

Hey little girl, I wasn't sure when I'd hear from you again, Clive replied, sending her an emoji of a bunny.

Well isn't it your lucky day then. What are you doing? Lola replied before putting her phone away as she heard Jake open the bathroom door.

"I'm not going to harass you to do it. Let me know when you've told him; I'll be seeing you," Clive said down the phone the next day. Lola had hidden in the laundry room, a place she knew Jake hadn't entered since she had moved in and called Clive, wanting to hear his voice. Lola didn't know what to say; all she knew is that she wanted out. Out of this town and away from everyone. She had the feeling of suffocation all over again. She couldn't figure out if it were this town or her life choices that made her feel so claustrophobic. She imagined her life with Jake, what it would look like, how it would feel then compared it to how Clive made her feel. What spaces he was able to put her in so easily and how he knew what she needed and forced it on her until she accepted. How he had stopped all the times, she had wanted to, but still pushed her limits and made her head spin with ecstasy.

"Cool, I think I just need some space. From like everything, I'm going to stay with a friend of a few days to just clear my head. This isn't what I was expecting, and I just need some time," Lola replied, holding her breath and hoping Clive was prepared to give her what she wanted.

"That makes sense. Just remember, Daddy

will be here for you when you decide," he said before hanging up the phone. *He is a real Daddy*, Lola involuntarily thought as she put her phone back in her pocket.

"Jake?" Lola called through the house, waiting as she heard footsteps coming from the living room.

"Yep," Jake replied, sticking his head out from behind the wall. Lola just smiled at him; he was too lovely, the kind of nice that annoyed her. It had been hot while they were fighting bad guys together, but now she was the bad guy, and he didn't even know it.

"My head isn't in the right place, and I kinda just want to get out of this place, out of this town and away from everyone for a few days," Lola said, making Jake's eyes narrow and become serious. He stepped out from behind the wall and looked at her, waiting for her to explain what was going on.

"What's going on with you?" Jake asked, crossing his arms in front of his muscled chest. Lola just looked around, fixing her eyes out the window.

"I didn't come back for this. I came back to sell drugs Jake, and now I'm in this happy little white picket fence life, and I just don't know if it's what I want. I need something more," Lola said, speaking honestly. Jake just snorted and shook his head.

"You've never been able to settle down, that's why you ran off the first time. I should have known you couldn't do it now either. Go, do whatever you need to do," he said, walking back into the living room shaking his head.

"I just need more," Lola softly said as she looked to her feet.

Chapter 13

What would life even look like, with Clive? Lola thought to herself as she walked through the park. The wind picked up, and she pulled her coat around her more firmly as the leaves swirled around her feet. She imagined living there with him in the cabin in the woods. He'd go to work, and she would stay at home, keeping the fire warm and cooking for him, getting fucked when he wanted and babied the rest of the time. *That's hardly the life I want either*, Lola thought as her cunt got wet with the idea. *Or maybe it is,* she added, noticing her body reacting. *How would I even hide it from Jake?* Lola thought. Jake would find out she was with Clive in about two minutes of their relationship being official and the thought of hurting him even more by living out her happy life in the same town as him made her nervous. *It's not like he hasn't killed a man before, what if that sends him over the edge,* Lola thought. She stopped at a park bench and watched the water of the lake. It was still, and calm, nothing like the turmoil she felt in her mind. *But then, the protection of a cop and the force, he couldn't say shit about what really happened that day,* Lola said to herself, biting her bottom lip and deciding that she was safe from that story ever getting out.

"I don't want to feel this way anymore," Lola said out loud, surprising herself. She heard a laugh come from behind her and turned around to see Clive in his police uniform.

"Then don't," he said, sitting down and taking her hand in his. Lola loved that he just took what he wanted.

"Easy for you to say," she said, glaring at him and pulling away, only making him laugh again.

"You sure do love playing hard to get, don't you. But you're not hard to get, just hard to keep," Clive said, whispering in her ear and licking her lobe. Pushing him away, or at least trying to, Lola wriggled in his grip as he put an arm around her and pulled her into his side, holding her there firmly.

"Now listen here, young lady," Clive started to say, making Lola stop moving, stunned by the words he was saying.

"Is that any way to respect an officer of the law. I might need to search you right here for concealed weapons," Clive said, groping her tit with his other hand, making her whimper softly into his chest.

"That's it, be a good little girl for Daddy," Clive said, feeling Lola's submission as she held still for him.

"How about you come around tonight. I'll send you the address," Clive suggested letting go of Lola and causing her heart to crave his possessive touch once more.

"I don't want to, I told you I need some time," Lola said, her sassy mouth taking over once again.

"Guarded little thing aren't you," Clive said, placing his hand on her upper thigh and squeezing. Lola just held her breath, slightly annoyed he could force her into her little space with just a look and a touch. She hadn't realized her hands were on his lap as her head rested on his chest, her eyes looking up at him and her legs wrapped in his.

"Are you planning to do something with those hands, or are you just being lazy?" Clive said, causing Lola to look at the hard rod that was resting in between her hands. Grabbing him roughly, Lola cheekily looked into his eyes as she licked her lips.

"You don't always get what you want, Daddy," Lola said, getting up to leave just to be pulled back down onto Clive's lap. She could feel him lift the back of her skirt and reposition his cock between her ass cheeks, pushing himself into her pussy through his trousers and making him grunt, happy she wasn't wearing any panties.

"Yes, I fucking do," He said, reaching under Lola's skirt and cupping her pussy, locking her down onto him with his strong arm. Roughly pulling his cock from his pants, he looked around to see that they were alone before leaning back and sticking his cock along her cheeks and jerking into her ass crack.

"Daddy, stop," Lola giggled quietly, worried someone might hear them. Clive just grunted as his dick was pushed against Lola's skin, lifting her up slightly and pulling her skirt to the side, her pussy lips being forced apart as he entered her.

"Daddy, always gets what he wants," Clive said, turning Lola's head around and kissing her passionately as he bounced her on his lap. His thick black beard soft against Lola's face as she was fucked, his hairy balls getting coated in the cum that dribbled from her cunt. Clive pumped her several more times before cumming hard, making Lola's pussy slippery and leak with his load as he pulled her skirt back in place and pulled himself from her. He wrapped his arm around her again as he held her to his chest as she began to cry, for the first time in years.

"Did I hurt you?" Clive asked, concern in his voice. Lola just shook her head and began to suck her thumb, causing Clive to wrap his other arm around her, holding her tightly and pressing her into him.

"I just didn't know I could feel like this," Lola said around her thumb, her little voice escaping.

"Feel like what, baby girl," Clive asked, stroking her hair from her face.

"Safe, Daddy," Lola replied, snuggling into him and closing her eyes as the first stars began to dot the sky.

Chapter 14

"Where have you been, I've been trying to call you for the last hour," Jake said the moment Lola walked into the house. It was late, she knew that, but she hadn't bothered to reply to his missed calls or texts. Sighing, she dropped her handbag by the kitchen bench and ready for what she knew would be a fight.

"I told you, I was out just to clear my head. I know that we have this whole thing going on, but I'm still a 28-year-old woman, and if I want some time alone, that's what I'm going to get," Lola said, sitting down on the couch next to him. Jake had felt this coming for a while. He had felt how removed she had made herself from him; if he was honest, he had done the same. After Kane's murder, things just hadn't been the same. They had both been walking on eggshells, wanting to escape each other, wanting some version of normalcy that never seemed to emerge from their relationship. He had tried to explain it to the girl he had been talking to online, saying that his relationship with Lola didn't feel right anymore but not knowing how to end it with her.

"Whatever, I don't want to fight about it," Jake said, turning the tv on and ignoring Lola who just continued to stare at him.

"Do you want out?" She quietly asked after some time. Jake looked down and wondered what the correct way to phrase his response.

"Lola," Jake said, looking at her like she was acting overly dramatic.

"No, I'm serious. Even since Kane and that day, things have been shit. Let's be honest about that and stop lying to ourselves like it's going to get any better," Lola said, standing up and walking to the kitchen. She took out a slice of chocolate cake and came back to the living room.

"We had fun; we were kids, then I left. You stayed, made this great name for yourself and maybe we were naïve to think that we were the same people we were back then," Lola said, happy that he didn't seem too heartbroken.

"I mean, I was only ever coming back to sell drugs, Jake," Lola said, looking at him with a smirk on her face.

"Yeah, and how did that turn out for you," Jake laughed. He looked up at the ceiling and sighed, feeling relieved she was not making this a big deal.

For the next four days, Jake and Lola slept in different beds. Lola worked with Clive, and Jake stopped making her breakfast. At night, Lola would look at real estate, deciding that she would find a place to stay of her own.

"What about this one?" She said, showing Jake the apartment near where Clive lived. It was small, but clean even though it was an older build and Jake nodded his head thoughtfully.

"I'd like to have a look at it with you. Make sure it has good bones. I could fix up a few things by the looks of it," Jake said, making Lola smirk.

"Once a Daddy, always a Daddy," she teased, passing Jake his phone, the photo of a girl showing.

"Oh, Tammy is calling," Lola laughed, ignoring the warning look Jake gave her and went back to looking at apartments when her phone rang.

"Hello," she said playfully, feeling more settled than she had in a long time.

"My my don't you sound happy," Clive said, down the phone.

"Well, yes, I am actually. I've seen some really decent places. Oh, I told Jake it's over," Lola said, remembering that she hadn't told Clive.

"How did he take it?" Clive asked, hoping that there wouldn't be any drama.

"Good, he is actually talking to Tammy Wilson again. He likes the boring ones after all," Lola said, giggling.

"Great. So, are you free now? There's a party I thought you might want to go to," Clive said making Lola's eyes grew wide.

"What kind of party?" She asked, wondering what kind of dress code would be appropriate.

"I've got a diaper in the car for you," Clive said, making Lola laugh and jump up. She walked into the nursey, happy that Jake had closed his door and was obviously talking dirty down the phone by the loud, deep tones she could hear coming from the room.

"What do you want me to wear, Daddy," Lola said, opening her cupboard.

"Bring you fluffy pink diaper cover, black sockies and white t-shirt, baby girl. Oh, and black binky and pink hair bow," Clive said. Lola collected her things in her bag and put in her blue bunny on her way out of the room.

"I'll text you the address," Clive said before hanging up. Lola grabbed her purse and truck keys before walking out the door, driving halfway out the driveway before she saw the address.

"I know that place," she said out loud with a smirk on her face. She had heard about these parties before. The ones where the town's secrets were laid out bare for all to see, the strictest privacy being enforced and discretion of the uppermost importance. As Lola drove to the location, she wondered who would be there, what kind of scandal she would see, and how Clive had been invited.

"Hey little one," Clive said coming to Lola's side of the truck and lifting her out.

"How do you know about this?" Lola whispered, unsure about why she was whispering. Laughing, Clive took her black bag in his hand and her hand in his other and walked her to the large wooden doors of the old plantation style mansion.

"I'm the one who is in charge of organizing it. I have been for the three years," Clive replied, taking Lola by surprise.

"Oh, so it if sucks, it's due to your shitty planning?" Lola teased, coping a slap on her bottom.

"Someone feels cheeky tonight don't you,

young lady," Clive said, pulling her over to the side of the entrance steps and out of sight.

"Lola, what you see here tonight, you can't talk about to anyone, but I guess me but only when we are in the house, ok baby?" Clive said seriously making Lola giggle.

"Yeah, I figured, Daddy," she replied, standing on her tippy toes as she saw the door open. Clive unexpectedly lifted her with one arm and carried her back into the light and up the stairs. They were greeted by two women wearing leather harnessing, their wrists cuffed behind their backs and gags in their mouths. Their nipples had rings through them with chains that connected to collars around their necks. Their make up was stunning, with dark, sensual smoky eyes staring back at Lola and Clive as they passed.

"They are gorgeous, Daddy," Lola said, turning in his arms and watching the woman standing still by the door as people groped them while they entered the mansion behind Clive and her.

Clive waited until he was in the main room before putting Lola down and pushed Lola gently onto her back, making her the center of attention and blush as people looked at her.

"You're fine little one, no one is going to do anything to you but Daddy," Clive said, showing Lola a soft side to his Daddy self she hadn't seen before. Taking her thumb from her lips and replacing it with her pacifier, Clive undressed her, exposing her naked body to the multiple onlookers. Amongst them, Lola counted the woman who owned the bakery and two of the bar owners, they were meant to be rivals, but they didn't look like they hated each other tonight. She saw multiple professors from the local university and the librarian. *I always knew she was too hot to actually be just a librarian,* Lola thought to herself as she watched the middle-aged woman have her pussy eaten by a much younger man while watching Lola be transformed into a baby in front of her eyes.

"There, my little Lola," Clive said, taking

Lola by surprise. She hadn't noticed that he had completely dressed her as she had been looking around the room.

"You can play anywhere you want, but there are a few other babies you might want to hang out with. Daddy is going to take you to them and then go and talk with a few people, ok?" Clive said, picking Lola up and giving her the bunny she was reaching for.

"There you go," he said, passing the major who was pegging the same boy who had just eaten out the librarian.

Clive passed more girls who looked like the ones by the front door, walking through rooms and occasionally stopping to chat with people Lola hardly recognized. As Clive walked into the playroom, he had specially designed for the babies that he knew who were attending; he stopped, his stomach knotting. Lola looked around to see why he had stopped and gasped as she saw what Clive was looking at.

"Jake," she whispered in Clive's ear just as

Jake looked up to see Clive holding Lola in her baby clothes.

"What the fuck?" Jake said, stopping the game he was playing with the baby on the floor and walking over to where Clive stood. Putting Lola down to stand on her own, Clive blocked the punch Jake threw at his face.

"Now just hang on there mate, we can talk about this," Clive said, trying to stay calm. Jake wasn't interested in talking and tried to strike again, this time Clive grabbing his hand and pinning it behind his back.

"I said, listen," Clive said, holding Jake firmly until he stopped struggling. Letting him go slowly, Clive came to stand in front of Lola who grabbed onto the back of his shirt.

"Well?" Jake said, shrugging his shoulders and shaking his head.

"Well, what?" Clive replied, unsure of what Jake wanted.

"Fucking explain this shit!" Jake said gesturing to Lola, who looked out behind her big

Daddy's back.

"You said he was a fucking creep, remember?!" Jake said loudly, making other people come to stand around them.

"Foreplay is an interesting thing like that," Clive said, enjoying his joke but making Jake even angrier.

"Why do you even care, it's not like you are here alone," Clive said, looking over Jake's shoulder to see that it is Tammy who he had brought to the party. Clive recognized the outfit Jake had dressed her in as one of Lola's, and he bit his lip, not wanting to escalate the situation further but annoyed that he wouldn't have bought Tammy something new.

"That's not the point," Jake said, feeling deflated.

"What's the point then?" Clive asked, seeing that Jake was no longer angry.

"Well, I loved her," Jake said, making Lola's eyes go wide.

"Sounds like it is past tense mate," Clive

said, stepping forward.

"Yeah I guess it is, it's just weird seeing all this, you know?" Jake said, looking at Clive for the first time in the eye. Clive nodded his head and shook hands with Jake as Lola peeped out from behind his back.

"Is that my pink sailor suit?" She asked Jake with narrow eyes in her little voice.

"Um," Jake replied, laughing.

"You never even liked it," he added before going back to sit down next to Tammy and began playing with her again.

"Daddy, I don't want to play here," Lola said, pulling on Clive's shirt.

"Yeah, I think that's a good call, baby," he said, taking her hand and leading her out back into the main room. He set her up in the corner of the room with her bunny and some blocks, coloring in and a movie on her iPad before he made his rounds around the party.

Chapter 15

"Did you have fun, little one?" Clive asked as he buckled Lola into the truck. During the party, he had seen how Lola was sitting in the corner watching everyone get their kink on and had known that she wanted to go home.

"Yeah, but I'm happy we are going now, Daddy," Lola replied as she played with her blankie and sucked her pacifier.

"It is late, isn't it. Daddy will get you home soon and tucked up in bed," Clive said, turning the truck on and driving onto the main road.

"I can't believe that the major was all like," Lola said making Clive laugh.

"And Ms. Williams from the library?!" She added, bringing her knees to her chest and pulling her blankie over her knees.

"Remember, though; it's a secret. The only

way we can have parties like that is because everyone plays by the rules and that means you need to as well," Clive said. Lola just nodded as she put her head back on the seat, feeling how Clive pressed the button to make her seat move backward so she could sleep on the drive home.

Clive and Lola settled into a life of work and play, surprising Lola with how settled she felt with him. She had spent her life running from anyone who got close to her, but with Clive, she didn't want to run. Every time she tried, he would just let her go. He didn't chase her; he didn't try to keep her, he just let her be with him without trying to cage her, and for that, she was genuinely grateful.

"Hey, have you sorted that list of most wanted? I need it on my desk," Clive said, popping his head around the corner of her office doorway.

"Um, no, not yet. Can I give it to you tomorrow?" Lola said, shuffling some papers as Clive walked into the room and shut the door, locking it behind him and pulling the blinds down.

It was late, later than either of them needed to be there, and the change over had the boys in the lounge waiting for something exciting to happen. Clive knew they wouldn't be interrupted as he slowly walked over to Lola, taking his belt off.

"No, I said I need it now," Clive said, repeating himself as he looped the belt around Lola's neck and pulled it firmly, collaring her.

"Get up on this desk," he instructed, lifting his arm, pulling up to her feet. She crawled onto her desk, her knee-length skirt being pushed up by Clive's hand before bringing it back down firmly on her ass, making her gasp loudly.

"Oh, baby, I wouldn't make so much noise. Not unless you want the boys to come in and see you being spanked like the naughty girl you are," Clive said, striking her again. This time he pulled her panties down roughly around her mid-thigh and as he continued to hold his belt in one hand choking Lola, her over spanked her ass red.

"Shake your ass for Daddy," Clive instructed, letting the belt go and walking behind her, spreading her ass cheeks apart and spitting onto her pussy before licking her with his fat tongue making sure she was completely wet from clit to asshole. Lola tried to stay still but pushed herself against his face wanting him deeper inside of her as he teased her with his tongue, tasting her sweet honey.

"Such a beautiful girl," Clive said, pulling her legs back and making her stand on her heels as she was bent over the desk.

"Are you going to stay a sweet girl, or does Daddy have to fuck you into submission?" Clive said, letting his pants drop to the floor and pulling his eager cock from his tight briefs.

"I've wanted to let this big boy worm his way inside of you all day," Clive whispered as he pushed into Lola, covering her mouth with his hand while his other one rubbed her clit as his cock filled her.

"Yeah, there it is, that soft, squishy warm honey pot, give it to Daddy," Clive groaned as he fucked Lola slowly, deliberately pulling out until his tip was being squeezed as Lola's pussy muscles contracted around it.

"Who is Daddy's good little girl," Clive said as he pushed back into her, watching as her head dipped and her breathing coming in short, shallow gasps as he pushed into her hilt.

"Can you feel Daddy. Can you feel it here," Clive said, taking his hand from her clit and feeling for his cock as it pushed out her tummy.

"Yeah you can, can't you. Daddy can feel it, feel how I own you," he said before pumping her harder and faster.

"Remember how the major took that gagged whore? That's how Daddy wants to fuck you today, little one," Clive said, pushing Lola's head down onto the desk and lifting his leg onto the table to get inside of her more forcefully. Lola just lay on the table, getting fucked and cumming more times she could keep count of as Clive pounded her behind. Groaning as he exploded inside of her, Clive pulled out and grabbed Lola by the back of her head.

"Get me down your throat," Clive said, burying his cock in Lola's open mouth, enjoying that he had taught her so well. She sucked him, her lips closing around his heavy rod, making her have to hold his balls in her hand to keep him in her mouth.

"Yeah, Daddy's got a big boy hasn't he, and you're going to make him very happy," Clive said, feeling Lola massage his hairy balls in her small hands. Suddenly pulling out, Clive let his cock swing as he walked to Lola's bag and took out the big pink dildo with the suction on the base, spitting on it and walking back to her. He took her office chair and stuck it to the middle before taking her hand and lifting her to her feet.

"Sit on it," Clive said, standing back and stroking his hard shaft as he watched her lower herself onto the dildo.

"Bounce, make those titties shake," Clive instructed, reaching for her tits and jiggling them, slapping his cock against her until she reached a rhythm he was happy with.

"Now finish Daddy off," Clive said, pressing his tip to Lola's lips and parting them slightly, taking his time, watching how she kissed him. He ran his cock over her mouth, shaking his head when she opened her mouth for him. He didn't want her to be so willing; he wanted to have to fight her today.

"Close your eyes," Clive ordered, slapping her face with his cock as she fucked herself on the dildo. Her legs were getting tired, he could tell by the slowing of her bouncing and picking her up under her arms, he carried her to the couch along a wall and laid her down. He pulled her panties down and placed them in her mouth as he ran his cock over her cheek, making her face wet with his mark.

"Daddy little princess," Clive grunted as he came on her panties, watching his cum drip from the edge of her panties and onto her lips.

"Lick your lips for me," he ordered, pulling the panties from her mouth and drying his cock off with them before sliding them back up Lola's thighs and over her pussy.

"Keep your eyes shut," he said, slapping Lola's tits when she tried to open them.

"Yes, Daddy," Lola said, she felt the wetness from her saliva mixed with cum press into her cunt by the pull-up Clive was making her wear over the top. He stood over the top of her, looking down at a woman he couldn't believe loved him as much as she did.

"I love you, Lola," Clive said, walking over to get his trousers and pull them back on. Lola opened her eyes, unsure of how to process the words in her current headspace.

"Just give me a minute," she said, making Clive laugh.

"It's all good baby, let Daddy take you home and look after you," Clive said, picking Lola up and catching her as her legs gave way.

"Daddy, I think you fucked my abs away," she said giggling as she held her tummy, sore from the hard fuck he had just given her.

Going out the back exit, Clive carried Lola to his

truck and buckled her in.

"I feel like you deserve this," Clive said, passing Lola a box wrapped in pink paper and a big silver bow.

"Can I open it now, Daddy?" Lola asked, shaking the box in her hands, wondering what was inside.

"Yeah you can," Clive said, jumping in the driver's seat and leaning over to kiss Lola's forehead. Lola ripped the at the paper as Clive drove to his cabin in the woods. Although Lola had bought her own apartment, she had decided to make it an investment and rented it out to three college students who paid her handsomely for the privilege. Opening the box, Lola saw that it was the colorful Lama stuffie she had been obsessed with since she had seen it arrive in the toy store they passed on their way to work.

"Daddy!" Lola squealed, hugging his arm and making him swerve as he drove.

"Woah, little one, be careful, Daddy still needs to drive!" Clive said, placing his arm out and over her body, not wanting to be hurt if she had caused him to have an accident.

"Sorry, Daddy," Lola said, instantly playing with her new stuffie and reaching into her bag to look for her bunny.

"It's here baby, remember Daddy took it out of your bag this morning when you tried to take it into work?" Clive said, pulling the blue rabbit from the side pocket of his truck.

Lola played for the whole drive home, talking to each the toys in her little voice and making sure they were friends. Clive played along, enjoying how comfortable she was in her little space. Pulling into the newly paved driveway of their cabin home, Clive swung the truck around and parked it in front of the door and unbuckled Lola before he got out and walked around to her side.

"Come to Daddy," Clive said, catching Lola as she jumped into her arms, both stuffies also coming and knocking into Clive's face.

"Good thing you are so cute," he said, carrying her inside.

"Daddy, Phoebe said she wants dino nuggies," Lola said, as Clive put her on the sofa and pulling her blouse and skirt off.

"I have a feeling that you want nuggies and are making Phoebe say she wants them, so I say yes because you know it's not dinner time yet. Did Daddy make you hungry after the workout I just gave you?" Clive said, causing Lola to roll onto her back as she giggled getting caught out.

"That's what I thought," he said, taking his clothes off and collecting both his and Lola's clothes in a pile and throwing them in the laundry basket.

"Come here, baby girl, you need a bath," Clive said, walking into the bathroom, followed by Lola who was busy trying to take down her pull up and panties.

"When will you learn little one, you are too little to manage this," Clive said, sitting her on his lap and undressing her before helping her into the bath.

"Bubbles, Daddy?" Lola asked, pouting

when Clive shook his head no.

"Oh baby, you little grumpy thing," he said, sitting in the tub behind her and beginning to wash her pussy.

"Daddy, it hurts," Lola said, pulling away from him. Clive reached over to the cupboard, taking out Lola's favorite duck washcloth and used that on her pussy, patting her gently and making her giggle.

"That's better isn't it, little one," Clive loving said, watching as Lola came to sit in his lap as he washed her clean.

"Yes, Daddy," Lola replied, closing her eyes and resting against Clive's bear-like body.

"You can't fall asleep yet," he said, standing up and letting the water drip from his cock onto her lips, watching as Lola's lips parted obediently. Laughing, Clive just took her hands from his thighs and put them back in the water.

"I was honestly just getting out of the tub little one, but you are such a good girl for Daddy. But not right now, right now I want to get you ready for bed and wrap you up in my arms," Clive said, stroking her cheek as his cock rested against her face, poking into her cheek and lips.

"Ok, Daddy," Lola said, going back to play with her bath toys, wriggling her arms and legs as Clive pulled her from the water.

"Daddy, I wasn't finished," she whined, copping a stern look from Clive. He carried her wet body in his arms as he took a new towel from the open shelves Lola had convinced him he needed and wrapped her in the large bath sheet.

"Go and stand by the fire, little one, Daddy will be there in a minute," he said, as he began to trim his beard. Nodding, Lola let her towel drag through the cabin until she reached the fire, warming her hands and dropping the towel the moment she was in front of its warmth.

"Baby!" Clive exclaimed, coming into the room and seeing her naked body silhouetted by the flames. Lola turned her head to see he had her bottle and diaper in his hand and quickly walked to where he was sitting, laying down, wanting her diaper on.

"Oh, you aren't going to fight Daddy tonight? That's a first," Clive said, tickling Lola's tummy and putting her diaper on before cradling her in his arms and feeding her the milky bottle.

"Daddy, what's this taste?" Lola said, noticing that her milk tasted different tonight.

"It's a new protein I'm trying, do you like it," Clive asked, giving Lola time to think before nodding her head and suckling on the nipple of the bottle as she nursed.

"Finished!" Lola said, flinging her arms up and trying to crawl out Clive's embrace as she finished her bottle.

"Hold on, little monster, last time you ran away after your bottle you had a tummy ache, do you remember that?" Clive said, holding her firmly against his torso. He had put on grey sweat pants, his long rod soft under Lola's padded bottom, but his chest bare and hair tickling Lola's check.

"You need to get dressed, Daddy, or you'll catch a cold," Lola said, repeating the words Clive had repeatedly told her.

"Is that so?" He said, wrapping her in a blanket before going to the bedroom and putting on a sport branded t-shirt and hoodie. That was the thing Lola loved about Clive. He had the most expensive wardrobe she had ever seen. From his sneakers to his cowboy hat, Clive never seemed to be lost for cash and enjoyed spending money on designer products and expensive tech gadgets without batting an eyelid.

"Cute, Daddy," Lola said giggling and lifting her arms to be held.

"Your turn, princess," Clive said, letting Lola crawl into the nursery they had made. Crawling to the blanket fort, she had built the previous night, Lola sat in the middle and watched as Clive took her orange onesie out and came to sit in her fort.

"Daddy, there's a password you have to say!" Lola said playfully trying to push him away.

"Is it, Daddy is the best?" Clive said, pulling Lola's arms through the long sleeves of the onesie.

"No," Lola laughed, standing up so Clive

could clip the three clips along her pussy shut.

"Is it, Daddy now has his little girl finally ready for bed?" Clive said, watching her. Lola shook her head, her hair flying before he pulled her onto his lap and put her hair in a messy ponytail.

"It's, Daddy, I know you took over my operation, and I'm cool with that. And also, I love you too," Lola said, kissing Clive full on the mouth, taking him by surprise. Wrapping her arms around his neck, Lola pushed her body into his, her tits rubbing against his chest and her diapered covered pussy dropping onto his cock as she relaxed facing him, her legs wrapping around his waist and resting her hands behind her, pushing herself into him.

"How did you know?" Clive said, looking at her, surprised but relieved she didn't seem to care.

"I just put two and two together. You are suddenly having all this cash, and then the bikers who had tried to take over the grocery store suddenly leaving town. Plus, I saw the paperwork that you signed for the purchase of the store. You overpaid, just saying," Lola said, smirking as she watched Clive become speechless.

"You know it's rude to go through people's private things, baby girl," Clive said, flexing his forearm and grabbing the back of her head, pulling her forward and resting her pussy against his hardening cock.

"I wasn't going through your things; I was filing. I filed that under, special secrets," Lola giggled, wrapping her arms around Clive's neck again as he rubbed her puffy, padded bottom.

"You're just as naughty as me, Daddy," Lola said as Clive stood up, Lola clinging to him like a monkey.

"Where are we going, Daddy?" Lola asked as he carried her out of the nursery.

"Well, you just told me you were a naughty girl, didn't you, sweetheart?" Clive teased, kissing Lola's cheek and the tip of her nose.

"No, I said you were naughty!" Lola giggled as Clive threw her down on his bed.

"Hmm, that's not what I heard. I heard that you were a naughty girl. And do you know what happens to naughty girls?" Clive said, tracing Lola's nipples with his fingertips until they were hard and poking through the material of her onesie.

"No, Daddy," Lola said, biting her bottom lip. Clive smirked a wicked grin as he pulled his sweats down.

"Naughty girls get fucked," he said, rolling her over, ripping open the clips of her onesie and pulling her diaper off her.

"Yeah, Daddy's naughty girl," Clive said, spanking her ass and watching as she squirmed, the diaper still between her thighs pressing against her hard clit as Clive positioned himself ready to take her from behind.

Who is Tina Moore?

Tina Moore has enjoyed the lifestyle of a Mommy Domme for several years. She began exploring kink and BDSM in her youth and found her love of being a strict Mommy Domme in early 2000. Tina Moore is now an author of many MDLG, DDLG and ABDL themed novels.

Follow her on:

Author Page on Amazon

Instagram @tinamoore.kdp